SPECIAL MESSAGE TO READERS

THE ULVERSCROFT FOUNDATION

(registered UK charity number 264873)

was established in 1972 to provide funds for research, diagnosis and treatment of eye diseases. Examples of major projects funded by the Ulverscroft Foundation are:-

- The Children's Eye Unit at Moorfields Eye Hospital, London
- The Ulverscroft Children's Eye Unit at Great Ormond Street Hospital for Sick Children
- Funding research into eye diseases and treatment at the Department of Ophthalmology, University of Leicester
- The Ulverscroft Vision Research Group, Institute of Child Health
- Twin operating theatres at the Western Ophthalmic Hospital, London
- The Chair of Ophthalmology at the Royal Australian College of Ophthalmologists

You can help further the work of the Foundation by making a donation or leaving a legacy. Every contribution is gratefully received. If you would like to help support the Foundation or require further information, please contact:

THE ULVERSCROFT FOUNDATION
The Green, Bradgate Road, Anstey
Leicester LE7 7FU, England
Tel: (0116) 236 4325
website: www.foundation.ulverscroft.com

THE MIDWIFE AND THE MURDER

After finding a body in the woods, post-war midwife Maudie Rouse takes a turn as an amateur sleuth, questioning the residents of the sleepy village of Llandyfan — between births and cups of tea — in a quest to track down the murderer. The brief disappearance of little Polly, and her subsequent refusal to talk to anyone, is somehow connected with the murder, Maudie is sure — as is the sinister Mr Smith, a travelling salesman. As Maudie edges closer to the truth, will she be next on the murderer's list?

CATRIONA McCUAIG

THE MIDWIFE AND THE MURDER

Complete and Unabridged

LINFORD
Leicester

First published in Great Britain

First Linford Edition
published 2014

A catalogue record for this book is available from the British Library.

ISBN 978–1–4448–2049–2

Published by
F. A. Thorpe (Publishing)
Anstey, Leicestershire

Set by Words & Graphics Ltd.
Anstey, Leicestershire
Printed and bound in Great Britain by
T. J. International Ltd., Padstow, Cornwall

This book is printed on acid-free paper

1

'Of course, it would have to be me who found the body!' Maudie Rouse muttered. 'As if I didn't have enough to do, what with three expectant mothers on my list, and two recently delivered women to keep an eye on.' If only she'd taken the long way round, past the church, the corpse would have been left for someone else to find, but she'd been in a hurry and had chosen the footpath through the woods instead.

Shocked, she attempted to make sense of what lay half-hidden by the undergrowth. As a nurse she'd seen plenty of dead bodies in her time, and laid out quite a few, as well. So finding this one wasn't as bad for her as it might have been for someone less experienced. She had to admit it was a bit of a shock to see the man's face, though; all purple and bloated like an overripe plum, with his tongue protruding.

'Police!' she thought, trying to suppress a shudder. 'I must call the constable!' That left her with a dilemma. Should she keep going in the same direction, and ring up from the call box at the crossroads? She looked at the woods ahead. Who knew what lurked there? Suddenly she found herself shaking, like an old man with the palsy. Turning her bicycle, she stumbled back the way she had come, until she reached flat land again and could mount the machine. Pedalling furiously, she reached the Bassett farm at last. Oliver Bassett was in the farmyard, tinkering with his old tractor.

'Hello, Nurse! Forget something, did you?'

'There's a body!' she gasped. 'Up there on the footpath!'

'Oh, aye? What sort of body? Some old sheep, mebbe?'

'A man. Strangled. Better call the constable. Before he gets away. The murderer, that is. The body won't get up and walk away.' She knew she was babbling, but suddenly the full enormity of what she had seen struck her like a blow. Farmer Bassett straightened up and lumbered towards her.

'I reckon I can do that, Nurse. Meanwhile, you come along with me and my Alice will make you a good strong cup of tea. That's what you need, after what you've seen.'

It was warm in the farm kitchen, and Mrs Bassett was there, still wearing the same old boots and the wraparound apron that Maudie had seen earlier.

'A body!' she marvelled. 'Fancy! Well, I reckon you could do with a nice cuppa after seeing a sight like that. Who was it, then? Anyone we know?'

'I've never seen him before in my life,' Maudie told her, wrapping her shaking hands around the steaming cup.

Their married daughter came into the room then, cradling her new baby. 'I thought you'd left long ago, Nurse,' she said, sliding into a chair beside the big scrubbed table.

'Nurse found a dead body,' her mother remarked. 'Nobody we know, the Lord be thanked. I reckon it's one of them DPs. There's plenty of them about.'

Now, in 1947, Britain seemed to be full of displaced persons as they were known, poor souls from all over Europe who had lost everything during the war and were now trying desperately to pick up the pieces of their shattered lives.

'Aye, that'll be it,' Farmer Bassett agreed, hearing this as he returned to the kitchen. 'We've had one or two chaps calling here lately, asking if there's any work going, which there ain't. That's to say, there's work in plenty but no money to pay for extra help. All we can do is give them a cup of tea and a bite to eat and send them on their way. Now, then, I've phoned the police station and the constable is on his way. He says you're to stay here, Nurse, until he's had a word with you.'

Maudie shuddered. 'I suppose he'll want me to show him the body, but the last thing I want to do is go up there again.'

'You'll be all right with Dick Bryant along of you,' Mrs. Bassett told her. 'Besides, whoever did the killing must be far away by now. You mark my words!'

'That may be so, but after this I'll never be able to go that way again, and it does save me time when I'm making my rounds. Once you get past the old folly it's all downhill from there until you get to the crossroads.' She shuddered again. 'When I think of how many times I've gone that way in the dark . . . ' She broke off, and little Mrs. Taylor clutched her baby a little tighter, causing him to whimper fretfully.

'I hear a car,' the farmer murmured. 'Must be old Dick, coming to collect you, Nurse. I'll help you stow your bike in the boot. After what you've been through you'll want to get back home and put your feet up and I'm sure he'll give you a lift.'

An ambulance came chugging to a halt behind the police car. 'You'll never get it up that hill, lads,' Bassett told them. 'Not with all them ruts and stones in the way.' He pointed to the stretcher that one of the uniformed men was busy unloading. 'You'll have to take that contraption with you on foot and hope for the best.'

'That's all right, sir. We know what

we're doing, thank you!'

'But do you know that old hill, that's what I'm saying,' Farmer Bassett muttered, refusing to be silenced. The constable regarded Maudie; not unkindly, she thought. Still, she could hardly be a suspect, could she?

She answered his questions steadily, her hands folded in front of her, just as she would have stood when reporting on a patient's condition to a doctor in a ward in her training hospital. That was after she had qualified, of course; no trainee nurse was permitted to address a doctor directly.

Yes, she agreed: the body was lying half in the open. How else could she have seen it? She hadn't been rooting around in the undergrowth. No, of course she hadn't touched the body.

'Then how did you know the chap was dead?' the constable wanted to know. 'And why do you think it was murder?'

'I'm a trained nurse, that's how. And believe me, all it took was one glance, and there was no doubt in my mind. You'll see for yourself once we get up there.'

Trudging along in the wake of the three men, Maudie was assailed by doubts. What if they got up there and the body was gone? How could she explain that to the law? 'Don't be a fool!' she told herself fiercely. Of course it would be lying there, just as she had left it. That was, unless she had disturbed the murderer and he had got rid of the body as soon as she had gone stumbling down to Bassett's farm.

'Did you say something, Nurse?' The constable slowed down, waiting for her to catch up.

'Just a bit out of breath,' she muttered, feeling foolish. A cry from up on the hillside told them that the ambulance men had reached the site of the murder.

Constable Bryant touched her arm. 'I'd like you to hang back for a moment, Nurse, while I go and see what I can see. Then I shall need you to come up and take another look, just to make sure that nothing has been disturbed since you were here earlier. Do you think you can manage that?'

'Certainly, constable.' Fortified by Alice Bassett's strong tea, Maudie felt up to the challenge. Besides, she would be safe enough with three burly men at her side. And indeed, when the time came, she was able to view the corpse with nothing more than pity, nodding and agreeing that everything seemed to be the same as it had been half an hour earlier.

'I'd like to know who did this,' one of the ambulance men growled. 'What's the world coming to, eh? Six years we had of war. Wouldn't you think people would be sick of killing each other by now?'

Shaking his head in agreement, Dick Bryant studied the body. 'Are you sure you haven't seen this chap before, Nurse Rouse? I don't get over this way all that often, unless there's trouble, but you're in and out of most of the houses, aren't you?'

'I suppose so, but I'm a midwife, you know. Most of the men I come across are the husbands of my patients, and a lot younger than this chap.'

'I daresay, but what about the fathers of those young women? Could this chap have come here visiting his daughter and a new grandchild, let's say?'

'I really don't know, but perhaps I can find out.'

'You do that, Nurse, and please report back to me, if you don't mind.'

'Certainly I will, Constable.'

Maudie's eyes sparkled. Had she heard aright? She had just been given permission to probe this mystery! Not only had she found the corpse of a murdered man, she was in a position to find out important information which would help the police investigation. She was a keen reader of Agatha Christie's detective stories; in fact, she had *The Body in the Library* on her bedside table at this very moment. What if she was able to discover a vital clue, or even to unravel the whole thing? A frisson of excitement went through her plump body as she thought of the possibilities.

2

Over the centuries the hamlet of Llandyfan had sprung up in such a way that it was now in two parts, separated by a long spur of wooded hillside. Ancient cottages dotted the long lane leading to scattered farms, and beyond them was a wider road meandering from a crossroads to the village proper. There, a concentration of houses, the Norman church and a few shops crouched in the shadow of the great hill.

Maudie moaned, thinking of the extra miles that were now added to her route, for she couldn't bear the thought of taking the footpath that provided a shortcut between the two sections of the community. This was irrational, she told herself, for all traces of the crime had now been removed and the killer, whoever he might be, must be far away by now. Still, the thought of trudging through those trees, where a murderer could be waiting to pounce, gave her the shivers. It would take a braver soul than Maudie Stevens to go that way again!

This morning she planned to visit one of her new mothers, Daisy Larke, who lived less than two miles away. There she would start her investigation.

When Maudie had rung twice, and pounded on the knocker, Daisy came shuffling to the door, looking haggard. 'Sorry, Nurse. I must have nodded off for a minute.'

'How is young Richard, Mrs. Larke?'

'Bawling in the small hours and half the day besides. I'll be that glad when he starts sleeping through the night. My Steve got up this morning cross as a weasel on account of being kept awake, and him having to go to work today. And look at me! It's wash day, this is, and here's me, limp as a rag.'

'The child will settle in time, Daisy. Meanwhile you must try to take things easy. Rome wasn't built in a day. Now then, got the kettle on, have you? The washing can wait five minutes while we have a nice cup of tea.'

Yawning, the young mother moved to the old kitchen range, while Maudie settled herself at the table, first removing an indignant cat from the seat.

'You don't have parents nearby who could give you a hand, do you, dear?' Maudie asked when they were seated at the kitchen table with a large brown teapot between them.

'I thought you knew my mum was dead,' Daisy said sadly. 'Two winters ago she went, or she'd have been here with me now.'

'And your poor father? Still in Gloucester, is he?'

'Why, no. He's here. Out the back. He couldn't manage all on his own, so Steve fixed up the old scullery to make a bedroom for him. It's not the best arrangement but at least I can keep an eye on him, make sure he's all right.'

Maudie sighed. No wonder the poor girl looked exhausted, up at all hours with a crying infant, and keeping house for her husband and father at the same time. Well, at least they could cross the old man off the list of possible victims.

Apparently the news of the murder had already reached the household. 'Tell me how you found that body,' Daisy said, her eyes bright with excitement. 'Do they know who it is, yet?'

'Not much to tell. I was pushing my bike up the hill and there he was, on the side of the track. I could tell at a glance there was no hope for the poor chap, so I turned myself around and rushed back down to the Bassett farm.'

'And you didn't see or hear nothing?'

'The police asked me all that. Mind you, I didn't wait around to hunt for the murderer! The next thing, it could have been me lying there.'

'Well I hope they catch him soon, that's all. We could all be murdered in our beds.' The girl shivered.

'I don't think there's any danger of that, my dear. The killer must have done what he came for. Why would he stay here with the police looking for him?'

'Steve was in the pub last night and people are saying it must be something to do with spies.'

'Spies? How could that be? The war's

been over for two years now.'

'Well, Fred Coppins, him that was in the Home Guard, he says p'raps the killer was over here in the war but he couldn't get back to Germany in time before it came to an end. He's been waiting for his chance to escape but this other chap finds out about him and threatens to turn him in and have him shot. So the poor chap has to be silenced, see, before he can go to the authorities.'

Maudie shrugged. 'It sounds a bit far-fetched to me. I shouldn't think they'd shoot a former spy after all this time. Probably they'd send him to prison for a bit and then ship him home,'

'Mind you, Dad has a different idea. He says, what if it's the dead man who was the spy, and that's why he was killed? P'raps someone's wife or sister died on account of him — in the war, like — and this was revenge?'

'I'd better be going,' Maudie said, standing up. 'I expect we'll know more once they identify the corpse.'

A fretful wail came from the bedroom, followed by a thumping on the other side of the kitchen wall. 'Can't you keep that young'un quiet, gal? How's a chap to get his rest with that going on, morning till night?' Daisy wiped a tear from her eye.

'Never mind him,' Maudie said. 'He'll have to get used to it. You go ahead and feed the baby, dear. I'll go in and have a word with your dad.'

'Oh, no, better not do that. He can be ornery when he's roused.'

'Never you mind. I can deal with him.'

After a perfunctory knock, Maudie sailed into the bedroom, where an unshaven man lay sprawled on a makeshift bed. He scowled up at her.

'Who the hell are you?'

'I'm Nurse Stevens, come to check on Mrs Larke and the baby.'

'Is that so! Then I hope you've told her to keep that nipper quiet. I've lain awake all night long listening to that screeching.'

'Come now, man! You're a father. Surely you remember the days when your own children were young and needed extra attention?'

'That's nothing to me. My wife saw to all that side of things, didn't she? Weren't my job. I went out to work to put food on the table, and she had the easy part, sitting home all day, with nothing to do. And why does a man bother having kids, I ask you? That lazy lump of a girl of mine never even brought me my breakfast. What do you think about that, hey? You women is all the same. Useless!'

Maudie saw red. 'I'll tell you what's useless, my man! That poor girl of yours has a new babe, and nobody to help her. She shouldn't even be out of bed yet! She should be enjoying her nine days' lying-in, not running about after an able-bodied man like you! She has the washing to get on with today, but are you out there drawing water to help her do it? No, you're lying there moaning, like a great fat ninny! I hear you think it's spies that murdered that poor chap I came across up on the hill. Then let me tell you this! Perhaps it's some poor woman who's been driven too far that's bumped him off!'

'Eh? What?'

'You heard me! Now just you get moving and give that poor girl a hand.

Next time I call in I don't expect to hear that you've taken to your bed, moaning and groaning, or I'll report you! And then see where you'll be!'

Maudie marched out and, snatching up her bag as she stalked through the kitchen, went to retrieve her ancient bicycle. Well aware that reporting the fellow was an empty threat — for who was there to report the fool to? — she regretted losing her temper. Her mother had often repeated the old saw that we catch more flies with honey than with vinegar. Horrid thought! But it would take more than honey to correct a lifetime of poor attitudes in a man such as Daisy's father.

* * *

Next on her list was a small boy, who was confined to bed with chickenpox. She was a qualified midwife and strictly speaking it was not her job to attend to other medical cases. However, the District Nurse was stationed at Brookfield, ten miles away, and the nearest doctor was even farther away, and it had long ago been decided that Maudie would see to routine cases in the Llandyfan district. War had taken many medical personnel into the armed forces, or to the big cities during the blitz, and country people had been left to manage as best they could.

Maudie's main problem was that some people tended to think of her as 'only' a midwife, skilled in bringing babies into the world and providing aftercare for the mother, but less knowledgeable about everyday illnesses. More than once she'd had to state quite firmly that she was a qualified nurse who had done her midwifery training after graduation.

Today, however, she was welcomed into every home she visited because everyone was eager to hear how she had discovered the body. Not that there was anything much to say, because she certainly was not going to describe the horrid sight that had her met her eyes. As it was, the bloated face had haunted her dreams last night and would continue to do so for some time to come, she was sure.

3

'My granddad's coming to see me, Miss!' The little boy, still flushed and fretful, tried to sit up in his rumpled bed.

'That's nice, dear,' Maudie said, feeling his forehead. 'Now, let's just pop this thermometer under your tongue, and then you can sit in your chair for a minute while Mummy and I change your sheets. Has your father far to come, Mrs Harper?'

'He's Bill's dad, not mine, Nurse. And you know him, surely. He keeps the Royal Oak out on Church Lane.'

Maudie frowned. 'I thought the landlord's name was Frost.'

'So it is. Bill's Mum was married twice, see? Her first husband died when Bill was just a toddler. A thatcher, he was. Killed falling off a roof. After Fanny wed Len Frost she wanted Bill to keep the surname he was born with, in memory of his real dad, see?'

'And very right and proper, too.'

'So Len is a sort of step granddad to Danny here, but the boy is too young to understand stuff like that. He worships his granddad Len, don't you, love?'

'He brings me comics,' the child murmured, now relieved of the thermometer. 'The *Dandy*, or the *Beano*. Maybe both this time, cos I'm sick.'

Maudie laughed. Everybody knew Len Frost: a burly, genial man, who presided over the Royal Oak in Church Lane. Obviously, then, he was not the unknown victim. But that did not absolve him from being the murderer, did it? Easy-going he might be, but judging by all the reports she had read in the *News of the World*, not all criminals were wild-eyed monsters with blood dripping from their claws. Anyone might kill, if pushed too far.

But what cause could Len Frost have for stabbing the stranger? Maudie knew from reading Agatha Christie's books that there had to be a motive. Her murderers always had one of those, usually revealed at the end of the book. Presumably the author knew from the outset how the story would turn out, whereas Maudie did not possess a crystal ball.

No, the idea of Len being the murderer was nothing more than a fantasy on her part, like those misleading clues that were sprinkled throughout the mystery books. Red herrings, they were called, weren't they? In the unlikely event that Len had snapped, he might have felled the stranger with a blow right there in the pub; throttled him, even. Why follow him into the countryside to kill him? It made no sense.

'Nurse! Nurse!'

She came to with a start. 'Yes, Danny; what is it?'

'I said: can I get up today?'

'Not just yet, dear. Your temperature is still up a little, but we'll see how you are when I look in again tomorrow. Is he drinking plenty of fluids, Mrs Harper?'

'Oh, yes. Granddad brought you a bottle of Lucozade, didn't he, Danny?'

'That's all right, then.' Maudie made a great play of shaking down the thermometer. It was a good thing the young mother was no mind-reader. Len Frost a murderer, indeed!

* * *

'I'll see you to the door, Nurse,' Mrs Harper said, stopping for a moment to smooth her son's bedclothes, which he promptly kicked aside.

'I want to get up!' he howled.

'You'll get a clip round the ear if you don't do what Nurse says! Now sit still like a good boy and read your comic.'

'I read it already,' he complained.

'Then read it again! All finished, Nurse?'

'Don't you worry, Mrs Harper,' Maudie said, as she followed the other woman down the narrow stairs. 'They're always fretful when they're almost recovered, but haven't quite got there yet.'

'And don't I know it!' Her eyes lit up with anticipation. 'Awful about that young Willis girl, isn't it? The one who disappeared? Struck dumb, they say. I don't suppose she saw the murder, did she? Something must have happened to take away her power of speech like that.'

Polly Willis happened to be a patient of Maudie's, so she could not discuss her symptoms, or for that matter her progress — or lack of it. However, she thought that it was fair enough to dispel the notion that the child had seen something she shouldn't.

'Oh, no; she was back home before the murder happened, and I know that for a fact because I was called in to attend to her at the time. And, as you know, I found the murdered man and that happened later. There can't be any connection between the two events.'

'I suppose not.' Mrs Harper didn't sound convinced.

Maudie leaned closer to her, whispering in her ear. 'I think we should be careful about suggesting that Polly may have seen the murderer, don't you?'

'Why? I was only saying . . . '

'Do you remember those posters during the war? *Careless Talk Costs Lives?* We don't want anything to happen to Polly, do we?'

'What do you mean, Nurse?'

'I mean that if the murderer is still in the district and that sort of talk gets around, it could put her in danger. If the chap gets hold of the idea that she's seen him at work he may have to silence the poor child. Yes, she's saying nothing now, but we think that her silence is what we call psychological. One of these days she'll find her voice again and be able to tell what she knows, whatever that may be.'

'Oo-er!' Mrs Harper stammered, in best comic book fashion.

* * *

Intrigued by her conversation at the Harper home, Maudie decided to call in at the Willis house, despite the fact that it was a school day and the children would be gone.

'I decided to come and see how Polly is getting on,' she said, sitting at their kitchen table while her hostess waited for the kettle to boil. 'You must be worried about her. Has she shown any sign of talking, yet?'

'Not a word,' Helen Willis sighed, reaching up to a high shelf to bring down the tea caddy. Maudie noticed that it bore a picture of Queen Victoria. It probably dated from 1897, at the time of the old queen's diamond jubilee. 'I finally gave in and took her to town to see the doctor. My Bob wasn't keen; he said it was a waste of money — but what's money for, if it's not to spend on the people you love? To tell the truth, Nurse, I was afraid her brain might have been turned by what happened to her, and that's a fact!'

'And are we any closer to knowing what did happen to her?'

Helen shook her head. 'How can we be, when the poor little love won't speak?'

'And what did Dr Mallory have to say?'

'Nothing much. I suppose Bob was right; it was money down the drain for all the good it did. He peered down her throat and shone a torch in her eyes, and we were none the wiser. All he could say was, 'Send her back to school. When she's playing about with the other kiddies she may forget what's been bothering her and be brought back to normal.'

'And do you think that's likely?'

'No, I don't, Nurse Rouse. If she won't talk to her own mother, who else is she going to speak to? Mind you, sometimes I get so cross I feel I want to shake it out of her, and then I feel that ashamed I can't tell you. Something or somebody must have terrified the poor little mite, that time she went missing. I tell you, Nurse; my imagination's run riot since it happened, and I can't get no rest.'

'Never mind; you've got her safe at home again, my dear.'

The kettle whistled and Helen Willis turned away to see to it. When the tea had been made and the pair had full cups in front of them, Maudie spoke again. 'What about Lily?' she asked, referring to the other child of the family. 'They're close in age, aren't they? Almost twins? Won't Polly confide in her?'

'If she has, I don't know about it, and I don't want to ask. Our Lily's been jumpy as a cat ever since Polly disappeared and I've been trying to make out everything's back to normal. I reckon she's scared something will happen to her, too, poor little thing.'

'Ah, well, I suppose it will all come out in the wash,' Maudie said, quoting the homespun philosophy she'd learned at her mother's knee. 'Children are amazingly resilient, you know.'

'Perhaps it will,' Helen Willis replied, but she didn't sound convinced. In fact, Maudie could have sworn there was something like fear in the other woman's eyes.

4

Maudie was sitting comfortably on the ancient green bus, being taken to Brookfield for her weekly meeting with Nurse Julia McGrath. Ten miles there and ten miles back was just too far to cycle; and besides, she needed the break. As the bus trundled through quiet lanes, occasionally stopping to let a small herd of cattle pass by, driven by some rosy-cheeked countrywoman, Maudie was able to let her thoughts wander.

She knew most of the other passengers on the bus, and she was privy to all of their ills and many of their secrets. There was old Mrs Garson, knitting some brightly coloured scraps into what looked like a scarf, despite the arthritis that plagued her sorely. Little Mrs Fraser with her sad eyes, still mourning the loss of her little boy who had died of meningitis during the war. Jolly Mrs Langtree, who had given birth to three lovely babies since her husband's return from the war: a fair-haired little boy and sweetly pretty twin girls.

And what did all these women think about her, Maudie wondered? She was Nurse, there to be called on in their hour of need; and, she hoped, she could be seen as a soothing presence. She was no oil painting, she admitted to herself. Just a rather ordinary person, approaching middle age. She'd never been married — probably never would take the plunge now, so late in the day — yet she could understand the hopes and fears of her female patients, being a woman herself.

Maudie and Julia both worked under the supervision of old Doctor Mallory at Midvale. No doubt he had been a good doctor in his day, Maudie told herself with a sigh, but the poor old boy was getting past it now. He still saw patients in his surgery, which was just a room in his home, but he preferred not to make house calls unless they were absolutely necessary. He depended on the nurses to let him know when patients really needed him; otherwise they could be seen at the cottage hospital twenty miles away. What they really needed, of course, was one or two nice young doctors, but where to find them? That beastly war had swept so many of them into its giant maw, leaving much of the civilian populace to the ministrations of old chaps brought back out of retirement.

The bus lurched to a halt and a large woman clambered on, panting her way down the aisle to collapse into the vacant place beside Maudie. 'There you are, Nurse! I was hoping to run into you. I want you to tell me all about it!'

No prizes for guessing what the woman was talking about, Maudie told herself. She related her story yet again, conscious of ears flapping all over the bus. Even Bill Todd, the driver, kept looking back at her over his shoulder, eager not to miss anything.

'You keep your eyes on the road, Bill Todd!' Maudie's seatmate bawled. 'You'll have us all in the ditch and that body Nurse found won't be the only corpse round here. Tell you what, I'll come and sit beside you on the way back and tell you all about it. How will that be, eh?'

And that's how rumours get started, Maudie thought, resigning herself to being misquoted all over the county if she wasn't careful. 'There's really nothing more I can tell you,' she said at last.

'Aw! I heard they'd taken the chap away to do one of them topsy things.'

'An autopsy, yes, not that will tell them much. Anyone with half an eye in his head could see the poor chap was strangled. The police will be no further ahead until they find out who the man was. It may be they found some sort of identification in his pockets; but if they have, they certainly haven't told me.'

Which is really too bad, considering it was me that found the body, Maudie mused, but she didn't speak her thoughts aloud. Long years of nursing had taught her to keep her opinions to herself. Still and all, that Dick Bryant might know she'd be on tenterhooks waiting to know more. Hadn't he more or less given her the order to poke about to see what she could find?

She was glad when the bus drew into Brookfield, coming to a halt beside the old market cross. Hurrying down the tree-lined street, she turned in at the gate of an old dairy that was used as makeshift offices for various professional people. She grimaced, looking at the peeling plaster on the outer wall of the building. Brookfield had been out of reach of the bombing during the war, but building materials were in short supply and it was almost impossible to carry out non-essential repairs. Naturally, housing was the first priority when so many people in the cities had been bombed out.

Julia greeted her cheerfully. 'Come on in! I've got the kettle on.'

'Just what I needed to hear,' Maudie replied. 'And before you ask, no, I haven't solved the murder yet, and I've no idea who the mystery man might be.'

Julia smiled like a complacent cat. 'Oh, but I have! His name was Cyril Swain, and he was a visitor up from Devon.'

Maudie's mouth dropped open in surprise. 'How on earth did you find that out?'

'From Doctor Mallory's receptionist. I had to phone him to see about a prescription for a patient here, and the woman was full of the news. Apparently the chap had been staying at a boarding house here in Brookfield but also spending time at Midvale, and now the whole place is buzzing with excitement over it.'

'Well, I never did! And why has this only come to light now, I wonder?'

'According to Miss Holmes this Swain was supposed to be travelling around the area, just using the boarding house as a base. Mrs Logan, the woman who keeps the place, is a patient of Doc Mallory and of course Miss Holmes got the whole story out of the woman when she called in about her varicose veins. Swain went out one morning and was never seen again. Mrs Logan was a bit concerned when he didn't turn up for his tea, but she decided that he was a grown man who might do as he pleased, and he'd paid in advance, so it was really no concern of hers.

'Then a week went by and she began to

wonder if he'd done a moonlight flit, but when she checked his room she found that his things were still there and that's when alarm bells began to ring in her mind. She trotted off to the police and they took it from there.'

'But hadn't she heard about the murder? The news has been in the papers, and on the radio, too.'

Julia shrugged. 'Who knows? Perhaps she had, but why should she connect it with Llandyfan? You know what people are like in these little villages. They don't take much notice of what goes on outside their boundaries.'

Maudie held out her cup for a refill. 'But what was the man doing in Llandyfan, then? You answer me that. And how did he manage to get himself murdered?'

'Perhaps he was in love,' Julia said, with a dreamy expression on her face that made the practical Maudie want to shake her.

'What?'

'Yes. Let's say he met a girl during the war. They fell in love, but then they were separated. He was sent off to fight. Perhaps he was captured by the Germans, after the Dieppe raid or something, and sent to a prisoner of war camp somewhere. Now he's come back to find his lost love.'

'And she's fed up with waiting for him all these years without a word from him, so she ups and strangles him in a fit of the pique? Really, Julia! Your theory has as many holes in it as a worn-out colander. To start with, we didn't have any army or air force camps in these parts where he could have been stationed.'

Julia shrugged again. 'So what? Perhaps the girl was in the services too, but her home was in Llandyfan. Don't be so dismissive, Maudie. And I wasn't suggesting that it was the girl who did him in. It could be her husband, if she's got one.'

'We may never know. Now look, hadn't we better get down to business? I don't want to miss my bus and have to walk the ten miles home.'

'All right, if you insist. Well, I've got an expectant mum to add to your list. Susan

Freeman, married woman, twenty-six. They've just moved here from Lincoln and she's a bit worried because she had a miscarriage last year and she doesn't want it to happen again.'

'How far along is she?'

'About four months, I'd say. She seems healthy enough; weight gain, blood pressure all okay.'

'No cramps or spotting?'

'None that she's reported, anyway.'

'Do you want me to go and see her? We could pop over now, if you like.'

Julia shook her head. 'It's all under control, and she might get upset if it looked like I'd asked for a second opinion. She's anxious enough as it is.'

'Just keep an eye on her, then. Mind you, if you have any concerns at all, and you can't manage to get hold of me, do encourage her to see Doc Mallory. Better to be safe than sorry.'

'I suggested that, but she said she'd rather wait and see. Doesn't want to spend the money, I suppose. I tell you, Maudie, I'll be glad when this new National Health scheme takes effect next year. Then people won't have to do without badly needed health care for the sake of a few pennies.'

'There's a lot of doctors who don't agree with you, according to what I've seen in the papers. They say it will encourage malingerers.'

'Huh! More likely they're worried about their fees when their pay is doled out by the government instead of coming out of the patients' pockets. Well, I for one will be thankful when I don't have to go cap in hand to my patients to get my pay. You wouldn't believe some of the sob stories I get. One woman told me she'd had a shilling set aside for me, but her little boy had swallowed it. She'd given him syrup of figs and was hoping for the best! Needless to say I came away without it.'

Maudie laughed. 'Sounds like a shaggy dog story to me. More likely her old man squandered it down the pub and she's too ashamed to let you know.'

Somehow the two nurses managed to complete their work, aided by the stimulus of numerous cups of tea. Each made copious notes that would be transferred later to the official files. They discussed the idea of setting up monthly clinics in their respective districts where they would both be present to advise the patients who would come to them, rather than the other way around. They would have to get Doc Mallory's approval, of course, but he would probably be thankful to have some of the load taken off his shoulders and would not object.

In due course Maudie made her way to the bus stop, much refreshed by the time spent with her colleague. Much as she enjoyed her work at Llandyfan, she did miss the interaction with other nurses, something she would have experienced in a hospital setting.

It was only when she was on the bus, rocked half asleep by the rhythmic swaying of the vehicle, that a thought occurred to her. Although fanciful, Julia's notion of what had prompted Cyril Swain's arrival in the area could have had some merit, save for one thing. The man that Maudie had seen lying in the shadow of the trees, whose life had been so cruelly ended, could not possibly have served in the war. He was far too old for that.

5

Maudie had a small office in the parish hall attached to St. John's Church. It was a small room, hardly bigger than a walk-in cupboard, containing a table and two chairs, as well as a metal filing cabinet, all purchased as army surplus. She often thought that it would be more convenient to keep her files in the cottage she rented, but when she'd suggested this to the council she'd been overruled.

'You must be able to draw a line between your work and your leisure hours, Nurse,' she was told. 'Never take your work home with you. That leads to stress.' That was a laugh! Patients knew where she lived, and most of them thought nothing of rapping on her door when they had some problem that they believed couldn't wait. And of course she expected to be called out when one of her maternity patients needed her; such was the nature of the job.

Maudie was seated in this office, trying to make sense of the scrawled notes she'd taken at Brookfield, when the vicar's wife put her head around the door, rapping on the woodwork as she did so.

'I'm making coffee, Nurse. It's only Camp, I'm afraid, not the real thing, but there's some freshly made scones to go with it if you're interested. Do you want to come back with me now? Or I can bring a cup over if you're too busy to leave?'

'No, no, I can join you. I want to have a word with you anyway. I'll follow as soon as I lock up here. Can't risk letting anyone see my medical records, can I? Not that anyone but me could read my writing anyway.'

'Can't you type, Nurse?'

'Yes — with two fingers, anyway, but the ribbon on that machine is so worn out you can see daylight through it.' She glanced balefully at the ancient Smith-Corona on the table. 'Why is everything still in such short supply? The war has been over for more than two years.'

Joan Blunt sighed. 'I know. I went

shopping in town yesterday and there was a lovely set of china in one of the shops, patterned with pink roses. There was a big sign on it saying 'for export only.' How mean is that? Really, the powers-that-be need their heads read at times, I think.' Maudie licked the butter from her fingers with satisfaction. Despite the fact that the coffee she'd just drunk was made from essence, it was a welcome change from the various cups of tea she was usually given throughout the day. Sometimes that tea was so stewed she was sure her insides were permanently affected, and at others the brew was too weak to crawl out of the pot. She couldn't give offence by refusing to drink it, and she still remembered the days when she had to carry her own sugar with her, held in a screw of greaseproof paper. Rationing wasn't over yet, of course, but at least there was a glimmer of light at the end of the tunnel in these post-war years.

'Now then; what was it you wanted to speak to me about?' Mrs Blunt asked, handing Maudie another scone. 'I hope you're not going to tell me you've changed your mind about working at the jumble sale on Saturday? Of course, if it has to do with one of your mothers being confined, I'll understand.'

'No, no; nothing like that. There's nobody due for a fortnight or more, although stranger things have been known to happen. It's about young Polly Willis.'

'Ah, yes. She's still not speaking, poor child. I have her in my Sunday School class, you know, and she sits there like a little mouse, waiting for the cat to pounce. I'd give a lot to know what happened when she went missing.'

Maudie shook her head. 'I missed all the frantic activity when the men were out scouring the countryside, because I was at the Bassett farm all night, helping to bring Mrs Taylor's baby into the world.'

'And it was a terrible thing, Nurse, as I know because they sent for Harold, wanting him to pray for the safe return of the child. The mother was weeping and wailing, saying that Polly must have been kidnapped, and that she'd never forgive herself if the girl turned up dead, or worse.'

'Forgive herself for what?'

'I don't know. For not keeping a closer eye on her, I suppose, but she could hardly blame herself for the girl not arriving home after school. I mean, in a village this size it's perfectly safe for children to walk home alone; not that she *would* have been alone with her sister Lily being in the same class. But then, when Polly didn't turn up for tea, and then bedtime came and went with no sign of her, the fat really was in the fire.'

The two women were silent for a few moments, each thinking about the events of that night. Maudie had been welcoming a new baby into the world while the vicar's wife had been providing cups of tea and useless words of comfort to Polly's distraught mother.

'They got you to examine the child, Nurse. Weren't there any clues as to what had become of her?'

'The police asked me that, and as I said at the time, she seemed all right, apart from being cold and hungry. She hadn't been interfered with, so there were no worries on that score. She had a few bits of straw on her clothing, which made me think she might have been hiding in a barn or a stable, but she could have picked those up anywhere.'

'I did think that perhaps she'd been in trouble at school and was afraid to go home, but she's not the sort of girl to act silly in front of the teacher, or to answer back, and apparently that wasn't the case because Harold spoke to Miss Plummer about it, knowing she was as upset about the girl's disappearance as anyone else.'

Maudie chewed on her thumbnail while she digested this. 'I wonder why Mrs Willis kept wailing about Polly having been kidnapped? At least, that's what people keep telling me.'

Mrs Blunt shrugged. 'Well, you hear such awful things nowadays, don't you? And who can blame a mother for thinking the worse when her little girl goes missing? Anyway, all's well that ends well, as the Bard said.'

'You've been at Llandyfan longer than I

have, Mrs Blunt,' Maudie began, following up a new thought.

'Bless you, yes. We've been at St. John's since the year dot.'

'Then why are the little Willis girls so close in age? When I got to know them first I'd assumed they were fraternal twins because apart from their flaxen hair they don't look much alike. But according to the birth dates in my files, they were born a few months apart, although not enough to be single births. I wondered if my predecessor had made a mistake.'

'Ah, now I can shed some light on that. I'd forgotten you weren't here at the beginning of the war. Well, we had quite a few evacuees in those days, and a young mother and her little girl were billeted on the Willises. Polly was an only child and I suppose they felt that Lily would be a little friend for her.'

'Oh, I see! So Lily isn't the Willises' child at all. But where is her real mother?'

'Ah, that was so sad. The woman went back to London to see her sick mother, leaving little Lily here. She was killed in one of those big air raids. We heard later that a whole street was flattened, taking the poor woman and the grandmother with it. Lily stayed on in Llandyfan, of course. The Willises kept her with them when the war ended and most of the evacuees returned home; those who had home to go to.'

'That was generous of them.'

'I suppose there wasn't much else they could do. It was either that or an orphanage, and those are filled to overflowing. And it's just as well from Polly's point of view because the girls are closer than any sisters could be, and the Willises have no other children. I sometimes wonder why that is. I believe that Bob was slightly wounded during the war. Perhaps that has something to do with it.'

Because of patient confidentiality, Maudie could not tell the vicar's wife that Helen Willis had once consulted her on that very subject. She longed to get pregnant again, but without success.

'There's no reason why you shouldn't have more children,' Maudie had assured her. 'Your girls are living proof of your ability to conceive.' For some reason Helen hadn't been comforted by that, but had gone on to say that her husband was keen to add to their family, particularly sons.

'Who does he think he is, Henry the Eighth?' Maudie had quipped, but her little pleasantry failed to raise an answering smile.

'Well, I must be on my way,' she said now. 'Thanks for the coffee, and I'll be there on Saturday, bright and early.'

'Right you are, Nurse! We're hoping for a good turnout. We've had some rather useful things donated, including a hand-knitted jumper that is in good condition apart from being out-at-elbows. Someone could pull that down and knit it up again into something nice. It's a pleasing shade of blue and would make a nice pullover for some little boy.'

Maudie went out into the sunshine, wondering if she could pick up the jumper for her own use. The wool would certainly come in handy for knitting Christmas gifts. She hadn't asked for it there and then because she knew how strict Mrs Blunt was about not letting her volunteers snap up all the goodies ahead of time, leaving all the tat for the paying customers.

6

'Eh? What?' Maudie struggled to emerge from a dream in which she was in an air raid shelter, trying to attend to a woman in labour while outside the skies were filled with machines raining down death and destruction. Not yet realizing that this was peacetime, she dimly recognized that she was in her own bed, and the phone was ringing. She must answer it, for perhaps the part about the woman in labour was happening in real life.

'It's me, Julia. Can you hear me? This line seems a bit faint.'

'What's happening? Is someone in labour over there?' As far as she knew there was nobody at Brookfield close to her time but there might be some visitor to the area, caught up in the drama of premature birth, having misjudged her dates.

'It's my mam, Maudie. Da just phoned. She's been taken sick and they say it may be a stroke. I've to go to Ireland at once; I'm needed there.'

'I'm sorry to hear that,' Maudie muttered, meaning it, but wondering why it was necessary to call her now at four o'clock in the morning. 'Is there anything I can do?'

'That's why I'm calling. I'm off out of here at first light. If I get up to Liverpool I can catch the ferry over the water. Meanwhile I've to make arrangements for my patients here. I've been in touch with an old classmate of mine. She hasn't nursed since the war, of course, but she'll come as soon as she can get away, and do my home visits. There's a woman in the village who does a bit of home nursing and she'll look in on the bedridden ones until Mairead lands in.'

'And what about me?'

'Could you come tomorrow and take over the office here for a day or two? And maybe check on my old fella with the bronchitis? He'll need his kaolin poultice renewed and I can't trust the village woman for that.'

Maudie thought quickly. 'Yes, certainly.

None of my mothers are due in the near future and I only have routine visits planned. Mrs Blunt can let people know where I've gone, and if anything important crops up Doc Mallory will have to stir his stumps and trundle over here. Now, how shall I get the keys to your office? And how do I find the old chap with the wheezy chest?'

There was no getting back to sleep now, so Maudie pulled on her old Jaeger dressing gown and thrust her cold feet into backless slippers. It would be a busy day, so she might as well make an early start, beginning with tea, hot buttered toast and scrambled eggs.

* * *

Later, seated in Julia's office, Maudie contemplated the appointments book with satisfaction. Several people had telephoned to ask for home visits, none being in any way urgent, and these she had earmarked for the attention of the unknown Mairead. The home nurse, Mrs Faber, had reported in for her orders and had left again, humming cheerfully. She was a chatty sort of woman and it was obvious that the news of Julia's departure would soon be racing around Brookfield like a dose of salts.

Maudie decided to remain at the office until lunchtime in case any patients came in for a consultation, and after that she would pump up the tires on Julia's old boneshaker and make her way to the man with bronchitis.

She telephoned Doctor Mallory's office to let his receptionist know that Julia was away. It would be too bad if the man referred patients to the district nurse in her absence, rather than dealing with their complaints himself. The woman made the usual noises of sympathy, assured Maudie that she would pass the message on, and rang off.

A young woman put her head round the door. 'Oh, I'm so sorry. I was expecting to find Nurse McGrath. I'll come back another time.'

'No, don't do that. Come in, please. Nurse has been called away to her ailing mother but I'm Nurse Rouse and I'm sure I can help. Come and sit down, and tell me what's up.'

'Oh, you're the midwife from Llandyfan, aren't you? Nurse has mentioned you.'

'That's right. And you are?'

'I'm Susan Freeman and, well, I'm having these little twinges. My husband says I'm making too much of it, but he's a man, so what does he know about pregnancy?'

Maudie understood at once. 'I believe that you suffered a miscarriage last year? And now you're afraid that history may be repeating itself?'

The girl's face crumpled and a solitary tear rolled down her cheek. Maudie patted the examination couch beside her. 'Just hop up here, then, dear, and we'll have a look at you.' Moments later she was able to give the girl an encouraging smile. 'All seems to be well, Mrs Freeman.'

'Then why? I did have these cramps, Nurse.'

'And you also told me you had fried onions for your tea last night! I'd say it's your stomach that's rebelling, not Baby. I suggest you follow a more bland diet until he or she arrives.'

The girl slid off the couch, adjusting her garments in the process. Maudie noticed that she still seemed despondent, and surely it wasn't because she'd been told to forget about the onions.

'There's something else bothering you, isn't there, my dear?'

'You'll think I'm an awful fool, Nurse. That's what my hubby says, anyway. It's just that I can't stop grieving over the little one I lost. Mark says I ought to pull myself together. What's gone is gone, and now we have this new one coming to take its place so I'd better stop fretting or it could harm the baby.'

Maudie sighed. 'It's quite natural to grieve, and you're quite right; a man can't understand, no matter how sympathetic he might be. Now I've been in this job for a good few years, and I'll tell you something I've heard time and again from my patients. They say that a woman doesn't really come to terms with her loss until the day comes when her pregnancy would have come to its natural conclusion. Now the doctors will say that's an old wives' tale, but I believe it's true. It's all a matter of hormonal changes in the body, you see. Now in your case I believe that you became pregnant again quite soon after your loss, didn't you? So I expect that your hormones are still in an uproar.'

Mrs Freeman managed a smile. 'Thank you, Nurse. I'll try to remember what you've said. It makes more sense than what Mark has to offer!'

When the girl had left, Maudie mused on her belief that all some patients needed in order for the healing process to begin was a listening ear and a bit of reassurance. And both of those she could offer in plenty.

The next patient to appear was a middle-aged woman who wore an unhappy frown on her lined face. Far from expressing doubt that a strange nurse could help her as well as Julia McGrath would, the woman seemed delighted to hear that Maudie was a midwife.

'Then you must know about things

down there,' she said, waving vaguely in the direction of her tweed skirt. 'The fact is, I'm afraid I've got cancer!'

'Then why haven't you seen the doctor, Mrs Logan?'

'Doctor Mallory? Oh, I couldn't see him about this! He'd want to examine me, wouldn't he, and I couldn't have that! He's a man!'

Maudie didn't know whether she wanted to laugh or to cry. The thought of poor old Doc Mallory being a threat to this lady's virtue was highly amusing, especially with the doughty Miss Holmes acting as chaperone. On the other hand it would be a tragedy if Mrs Logan's reluctance to see a male doctor led to a terrible diagnosis.

Fortunately there was nothing to worry about and Maudie was able to recommend a simple treatment, utilizing Epsom salts. Delighted, Mrs Logan relaxed, and was inclined to chat.

'You're the one who found my Mr Swain, aren't you?' she asked, lowering her voice in case anyone might be listening at the door. 'It must have been terrible for you, seeing the poor man lying there dead like that.'

'Why, yes.' Maudie realized now where she'd heard the name Logan before. This was the woman who kept the boarding house where the victim had been staying. 'I've wondered about him since, of course, and so far the police haven't told me anything. Had he ever stayed with you before?'

'No, he arrived quite out of the blue, saying that Miss Sampson at the post office had recommended me to him.'

'And what was he doing here? He seemed to be a bit old for going on a walking holiday or going from church to church doing brass rubbings.'

'Well, it was all rather mysterious, Nurse. At first he said he'd known these parts when he was a boy, but if he had, then he had a poor memory because he didn't seem to know his way about at all. Had to keep asking me for directions. Now I've lived in Brookfield all my life so I know the old families, but he couldn't come up with a single name that meant anything to me. If you ask me he was up to something, though I can't hazard a guess as to what it may have been. I went through his things after I heard he'd died — well, I had to tidy things away before I could let the room again, didn't I? And shall I tell you what I found?'

7

Seated on the bus as it jogged its way to Llandyfan, Maudie tried to relax but it wasn't easy. Her mind was awhirl with the knowledge she had gained, although she had no idea what to do with it. Pieces of the puzzle were there all right but the answer to the conundrum was just out of sight, 'seen through a glass darkly' as the Bible says.

After leaving Julia's office she had gone to call on Eric Thomas, the elderly man with bronchitis. After knocking on the door of his cottage, and hearing him call out to her in response, she had stepped inside to find him seated in a rocking chair with a large tortoiseshell cat on his lap. When the necessary introductions and explanations had been made she produced the kaolin and clean cloths she had brought with her, and set about making the necessary poultice. When it was warming in the oven she pulled up a chair beside her patient, returning his shy smile.

'Make yourself a cup of tea, Nurse, if you fancy one,' he offered. 'Sorry I can't get up; I don't want to disturb Millie here. Like the rest of us, she's not as young as she used to be.'

* * *

'No, thank you, Mr Thomas. I'm awash with tea already and I have to cycle back to the village when I'm done here. Can I make one for you, though?'

'No, no. My neighbour comes in at twelve to bring me my dinner. I'll get one then. Well, no! You just sit there and tell me all about yourself. Married, are you? I expect so, a pretty young thing like you. If I was thirty years younger your chap would have a bit of competition, see.'

Not so shy after all, Maudie decided. She laughed at the silly old codger. 'No, I'm not married, Mr Thomas. I'm afraid I don't have time for that. Besides, I'd have to give up nursing if I was, and I enjoy my job.'

'Even if finding corpses goes with it?'

'Just as long as there aren't too many,' she countered, although she didn't consider it to be any laughing matter.

'I met him, you know. That chap,' Mr Thomas said.

Maudie sat up straighter in her chair, wondering what was coming now. Was this another of his jokes, perhaps? But the man seemed serious enough. 'Did you? How was that, then?'

'In the pub down the road. I goes there of an evening when I'm not laid up like this. Not that I drink much, Nurse. I never have more than a half; can't afford it, see. It's the company I go for. Have a laugh or two, maybe a bit of a singsong. A chap gets a bit lonely, all on his own.'

Maudie nodded. 'And you met that Mr Swain. When was that, Mr Thomas?'

'I reckon it was a day or two afore he got himself killed. Asking all round, he was, saying had we heard of a Nellie Patterson, what had a nipper about nine or ten years old. Plenty of nippers, we told him, but no Pattersons in these parts.'

'Did he say anything else?'

'No, just shook his head, like he was disappointed. I think he left after that. I didn't really notice, on account of Fred Mould started talking about his racing pigeons doing well in their trials, see?'

Maudie saw. 'That poultice should be ready now,' she said. 'I'll just go and see to it. We don't want you getting burned, do we? That'd do you more harm than good.'

She had left soon after that, promising to go and see him again. How she wished she could have been present to ask a few questions of Cyril Swain. 'Fool,' she told herself. How could anyone have known that the poor man was going to get himself done in? He was probably just one of thousands trying to locate missing relatives who had been swept away by the war.

Her encounter with Mrs Logan had been no more profitable. The woman had given the impression that she had discovered some vital clue but it was all hot air. Maudie had been delighted at first, but on hearing that the marvellous find was nothing more than a wallet containing photographs her elation subsided.

'What makes you think the photos are important, Mrs Logan?' she asked, trying not to let her disappointment show in her face. 'A lot of us carry family snaps with us, don't we? In fact, I have a picture of my parents on my bedside table, where I can see it when I wake up in the morning.'

Mrs Logan pushed a stray strand of hair back into its bun. 'There must have been some reason for him coming here all the way from Devon, Nurse. I just thought having those snaps with him might mean something.'

'Have you shown them to the police?'

Mrs Logan bridled. 'What, and get a reputation for snooping through my lodgers' things? Let that get about and I'd soon be out of business. No, the police didn't ask me if I'd seen any snaps, so I don't see what business it is of theirs. Like you say, Nurse, a lot of us keep photos by us.'

'I'd like to see them,' Maudie said.

'I don't have them on me, but if you want to follow me home . . . '

'I'm afraid I don't have time now, Mrs Logan, for I've a patient to see. I'll be back tomorrow, though, if you'd like to bring them in to show me.'

'I daresay I could, but you mind you keep it to yourself. Like I said, I don't want . . . '

'People to think you're a snoop,' Maude finished for her.

* * *

Now, waiting impatiently for the bus to deposit her at Llandyfan, Maudie wondered what significance the photographs might have, if any. She would have to ask Eric Thomas whether Swain had shown them around in the pub. But if he had, that hardly seemed reason enough to get the man killed. And who else knew that he had those pictures? She would need to ask Mr Thomas about the other men who'd been in the pub at the time.

'Think, Maudie, think!' she admonished herself. If she were Hercule Poirot she would make a list of possible reasons why Cyril Swain had come to the area, bringing photos with him, and why that should make someone want to kill him. People were still talking about possible spies 'left over from the war'; and even if that notion was fanciful, the answer could lie somewhere in the events of those dark years.

It might be a question of family honour. Someone had been a traitor to his country and Cyril Swain had been a private enquiry agent, determined to bring the man to the attention of the authorities. Either the traitor himself, or someone hoping to preserve his family's good name, had silenced Swain before he could reveal his discoveries.

Maudie had to laugh at herself. That sort of thing was all very well in books, but this was real life. It was more likely to be some sordid little tale of wartime misdeeds. Bigamy, perhaps, with a wronged wife attempting to trace an erring husband. With so many records lost in the bombing, that sort of problem would be hard to sort out.

Or possibly somebody with an eye to the main chance had been selling things on the black market. That sort of thing was still going on because many goods were still rationed, including food and clothing. Maudie had been approached more than once by someone offering her tins of Spam or nylon stockings off the ration — at a price, of course.

Yes, such things could well result in murder, but then why would Cyril Swain have been involved, unless he really was some sort of investigator? Should she go to the police and suggest this to them? She cringed at the thought of being laughed at, and dubbed some sort of modern day Miss Marple. Then, too it would mean exposing Mrs Logan's little misdemeanor, which she hoped to avoid. She must keep her ideas to herself until she had more to go on.

8

When Maudie returned to Brookfield the following morning she found a tall, dark-haired woman waiting for her.

'You must be Nurse Rouse? I'm Mairead O'Neill, Julia's friend from our training days.'

'Oh, yes,' Maudie said. 'How do you do? I'm so sorry I wasn't here to greet you, but that wretched bus was late again.'

'It never fails, does it? It's Murphy's Law. When you have a special reason for being somewhere on time the whole transport system slows down. I'm early because I arrived last night. I'm staying with a Mrs Logan in the village. Do you know her?'

'I do, indeed. In fact, she's on my list of things to do this morning. I have to drop in to see her.'

'No need for that. I'm ready to get started as soon as you've filled me in on everything, unless her treatment can't wait until I see her at teatime.'

'Thank you, but I have to see her on a personal matter. As far as her treatment goes I have advised her to take mag sulph sitz baths but she should be able to handle that herself. Perhaps if you just check with her that she's actually doing it? Right, then, let me put the kettle on and we can have a nice chat.'

'I've brought a packet of custard creams with me,' the other nurse said.

Maudie beamed. 'A woman after my own heart! Now then, tell me a bit about yourself. Julia tells me you haven't nursed recently; is that right?'

'Not since the end of the war. My husband served in North Africa, so I went back to hospital work for the duration. I gave it up when he was demobbed, though. Working twelve hours a night on the wards is hard enough without trying to run a house and cater to a husband as well.'

'He doesn't mind you coming to fill in here, then?'

Nurse O'Neill grimaced. 'Martin did

put up a bit of a fuss, so he did, but I took no notice. I'm looking forward to getting back in harness, even if it is only for a week or two. Did Julia give you any idea of how long she'll be away? I've only spoken to her the once, you see.'

'Same here. I suppose it all depends on how serious her mother's condition is. Now, I'll give you a list of home visits, but I'll go back and do Mr Thomas's poultice myself. His chest sounds much better and we can probably discontinue them after today. And my phone number is on this list on the wall in case you need to get in touch. Not that you will; you don't have any expectant mums nearing their time.'

* * *

Maudie arrived at Mrs Logan's filled with a sense of excitement. Surely the photographs would tell her something. The woman greeted her with a sour expression on her face.

'Oh, it's you!'

'Turned up like a bad penny,' Maudie quipped, putting her foot in the door to prevent it being slammed in her face.

'Yes, well, I forgot you were coming, and this is my day for turning out the lounge. Can't you come back another time? It really isn't convenient today.'

'No, I can't. I have to go back to Llandyfan and I don't suppose I'll be coming back here. The relief nurse has arrived to take my place, but of course you're aware of that, since she's staying with you.'

'Oh, very well. Come in, if you must, but you'll have to ignore the mess. Some of us have work to do.'

And I don't? Maudie thought, but she bit her lip and followed Mrs Logan into an overcrowded room in which every available surface was covered with knick-knacks of various kinds. The woman — or someone close to her — must have travelled all over the British Isles, for some of the mugs and vases were emblazoned with the words 'A present from Bath', 'A souvenir of Wales', and so on. Possibly there were Logan children who periodically sent gifts home to Mum.

'Here you are, then.' Mrs Logan thrust

a cardboard wallet into Maudie's waiting hands. She did not invite her visitor to sit down, so Maudie moved over to the window, the better to see what the packet held.

There were three snapshots inside. The largest one, obviously taken by a professional photographer, showed a young man in the uniform of a Royal Air Force pilot officer. Turning it over, she saw that someone had pencilled in the name Teddy. There was no surname, so presumably the chap was a member of the Swain family. When identifying snaps you don't include your own last name, do you? In fact, Maudie concluded, very few people identify family snaps, because they know who the subjects are.

The next snap was smaller, of the variety taken with a Brownie box camera. It showed a young couple standing under a tree somewhere, cut off at the knees. 'And a fat lot of good that is,' Maudie muttered, for the reverse side was blank. There was nothing to say who the people were, or where they had been snapped. The young man might have been Teddy, but the picture was slightly out of focus, and Maudie could not be sure.

Disappointed, she glanced at the remaining photo. It seemed to be a studio photo taken years before, judging by the twenties-style frock and cloche hat worn by the woman who held a baby on her lap. The proud father stood behind her chair, looking smug. It appeared to Maudie that he might have been many years older than his wife.

'Seen enough, have you?' Mrs Logan brandished her carpet sweeper as if prepared to do battle with an unseen enemy.

Maudie handed her the photograph. 'Who are the people in this picture? Could this be Cyril Swain, do you think?'

Mrs Logan snatched it from her. 'How should I know? This is a young chap, isn't it, and old Swain was white-haired and going a bit thin on top. You should know; you saw him, didn't you?'

Maudie forbore to say that the poor man's own mother wouldn't have recognized him in the condition he was in after the murderer had finished with him. 'I don't suppose you'd let me borrow these for a day or two?' she ventured.

'You suppose right, madam! They're not mine to lend. Poor Mr Swain! I intend to keep his things by me, safe and sound, until someone comes to collect them. I owe him that much.'

'If I could just have them for a little while, I'd like to show them to Eric Thomas. I'll be going there next, so I wouldn't have to keep them long. I'll bring them right back, I promise.'

'Oh, Eric Thomas!' Mrs Logan snapped, snatching the wallet from Maudie's hand as she spoke. 'Silly old buffer! What does he know? Blind as a bat and dotty with it, that's what he is. No, Nurse. You've seen what you came for, now I'll ask you to leave. I've beds to make and a stew to make. There's no rest for the wicked.'

With a sigh, Maudie left the house. Having met Mr Thomas, she had to disagree with the woman's assessment. His mind seemed sharp enough and she wanted to ask him if the girl in the photo might be the mysterious Nellie.

'That's just like Beryl Logan,' he

grunted, when Maudie had given him an edited version of what the boarding house landlady had said. 'She's the sort who grudges them poor birds the scraps off her plate. Not that it matters much. Like I told the chap, I never heard of no Nellie Patterson and I've lived in these parts all my life, man and boy.'

'And are you sure he didn't mention anything about why he was looking for this girl? Could she have been a missing daughter, do you think?'

Mr Thomas shook his head. 'Couldn't be, could it? Not with his name being Swain and hers Patterson.'

'Unless she was a married woman,' Maudie suggested. 'Perhaps she eloped, or there was an estrangement between her and the family all these years. Swain may have mellowed with age and decided to put things right between them. People tend to let go of old grudges when they're getting near the end of the road. That's something I've often seen while nursing terminally ill patients.'

'I suppose so, but who bumped him off, then, Nurse? The son-in-law? It don't seem likely to me. Why would he want to do a thing like that? It doesn't make sense.'

Maudie had to agree. 'I'm beginning to think we'll never get to the bottom of the poor man's death. Perhaps it was just a coincidence, and nothing to do with why he came here looking for the lovely Nellie. But all this is driving me mad!'

'Now you listen to me, Nurse! I can see this has you all of a tizzy, on account of you being the one as found the poor chap. That's enough to upset anyone, nurse or not, and you must have seen some sights in your time. My advice to you is to forget all about it now. Don't you bother your pretty little head any more. Leave it to the police to get to the bottom of it, and when they do you can read all about it in the newspaper, same as the rest of us. That's an order, now!'

'Aye, aye, captain!' Maudie said, grinning, but she knew she had no intention of letting go.

9

The change of scene had done Maudie a power of good, but now life must get back to normal. The patients of Brookfield had been left in Nurse O'Neill's capable hands and Maudie had to turn her attention to her own neglected patients. Not that any of them had suffered because of her absence, but she was like a hen with a brood of chickens, anxious to keep them all safely under her wing. She needed to check on those women who had recently given birth, and her expectant mothers had to be given the once-over to make sure there were no problems with their pregnancies.

Her mouth was dry by the time she reached the Bassett farm. That might have been due to her exertion in pedalling against a sharp wind, but the nearer she came to the scene of the crime the more disturbed she became.

'How is baby Taylor?' she asked, as

Farmer Bassett stood aside to let her enter the kitchen, which was filled with the aroma of freshly baked bread.

'Named after me, Nurse!' he announced proudly.

'Ollie for short,' his wife chipped in. 'Oliver, that's too much of a mouthful for a child that size.'

'And where is the young master, then?'

'I'm so sorry. Our Mary's got him out for a bit of an airing. If we'd known you were coming she'd have been here waiting. Never mind; you'll not say no to a cup of tea while you wait, I take it?'

'Unless you want to go up the hill and have a look around,' Oliver Bassett said.

Maudie shuddered. 'Now why on earth should I want to do that? It was bad enough the first time, and I'm still getting nightmares about it.'

'There's plenty who do, Nurse. They've been turning up in droves. Ghouls! One chap even followed me into the byre, wanting to know where the body had been found. The cheek of it!'

'That's right, Nurse, you stay away!' Mrs Bassett said, as she brought the teapot to the table. 'I wouldn't go up there now, not if you was to pay me a hundred pounds, and we used to enjoy a stroll up the hill of an evening, didn't we, Oliver?'

'I know I'm just being silly,' Maudie said, reaching out to take a rock cake from the plate the farmer's wife held out to her. 'The murderer is well away by now. In fact, he must have been long gone by the time I found poor Mr Swain. There's nothing to fear.'

'Ah, who can tell?' her husband remarked. '*As a dog returns to his vomit, so a fool returneth to his folly*. Proverbs twenty-six, verse eleven. And don't you laugh, Nurse Rouse! I read in the *News of the World* just the other day about some chap that was going about setting fire to things. It said he always stayed around to watch what was happening. That's how the police caught up with him in the end. Well, our murderer could be up there this very minute, you see.'

Fortunately for Maudie's peace of mind, Mary Taylor came bustling in just then, full of apologies. 'I've got him outside in his pram, for a bit of fresh air, like. I can bring him in if you want to give him the once over, except I'd hate to wake him when I've just got him off. Awake all night howling, he was, and surely he can't be teething yet awhile? I've tried bringing his wind up properly but nothing seems to help.'

'I expect it's just a bit of colic,' Maudie said. 'Have you been eating anything spicy, or overdoing it on the baked beans? That could affect the baby through your milk. I'll just have a look at you and then we'll chat about diet, shall we?'

'I'll be off out then,' Oliver Bassett said, lumbering to his feet. 'This is women's talk, this is. No place for a working man here!'

Her mission completed, Maudie stood up to go. Then a thought occurred to her and she sat down again. 'You've lived here for a long time, haven't you, Mrs Bassett?'

'On this farm, you mean? Ever since we were married, back in nineteen twenty-one. We had our silver wedding anniversary last year.'

'But were you a local girl before that?'

'Oh, aye. Born and raised two farms over from here. You don't get more local than that.'

'Then would you have known a Nellie Patterson, by any chance?'

'Patterson? We've never had any by that name in these parts. Not unless she was one of those evacuees. What about you, our Mary? Do you remember any such girl from school?'

Mary shook her head. Mrs Bassett turned back to look at Maudie. 'Why did you want to know?'

Maudie scratched her head. Should she say anything, or keep it to herself? But she would never get anywhere unless she baited her hook. 'I've been over at Brookfield, standing in for the nurse there while she visits her sick mother. Somebody told me that Mr Swain — the murdered man — had been looking for a Nellie Patterson, that's all. He'd been staying at a boarding house in Brookfield so there must have been some reason for him to come to Llandyfan. Why else would a stranger turn up on your hillside unless he thought this Nellie might be found in this district?'

Mrs Bassett shook her head. 'It beats me, love. I'll ask around a bit, though. Somebody at our church might be able to help. Of course, there's such a thing as married name, you know. The girl he was looking for might have been Nellie something else if she was here during the war.'

'I've said, Mum, haven't I? We didn't have a Nellie at school. I'd remember if there was, because I was a monitor and I was supposed to help the evacuees get used to the place.' A howl from outside made them all jump. Mary stood up, frowning. 'O, lord! He's off again. You'll have to excuse me, Nurse. If I don't see to him at once he'll work himself up into a right old lather.'

'Yes, yes. You see to his lordship. It's time I was on my way in any case. Thanks for the tea and cake, Mrs Bassett. It hit the spot nicely.'

'You're welcome, I'm sure. See you next time, Nurse!'

* * *

Maudie's next stop was the Larke house. She had to rap at the door three times before it was answered by a bedraggled Daisy. 'Oh, it's you, Nurse! Come in, please, and sit down if you can find an empty chair. I'm all behind this morning, like the old cow's tail.'

The kitchen was full of steam, and there were bundles of garments everywhere. Daisy's old father sat beside the stove, squinting at a copy of the *Daily Mirror*. He looked up, frowning, when Maudie entered.

'It's you again, is it? Mebbe you can get this lazy lump of a daughter moving. Just look at the time and me with no elevenses yet!'

Daisy wiped her brow with a sleeve that was already dark with moisture. 'I told you, Dad. I'll be with you as soon as I get this lot on the line, all right?'

'Let me give you a hand,' Maudie said, biting back a sharp retort that surely would not improve the old man's temper. 'You look all in, my girl. I'll turn the mangle while you feed those sheets in. Then I'll make your dad his elevenses, and you'll sit down and have a bite too, and no back answers!'

They left the old man grumbling, and when the laundry had been through the mangle Maudie took one handle of the wicker basket and motioned to Daisy to take the other. Maudie took over the job of pegging out the washing when she saw that the girl seemed too exhausted to heft the heavy wet sheets.

'How is little Richard doing, Daisy? Is he sleeping any better?'

Daisy sighed. 'He wants to do everything the wrong way round, Nurse. He won't settle at night, which means he sleeps all day! That's a good thing in a way because I can get on with my chores now, but I'd give anything for a good night's rest! I've tried him on gripe water but it doesn't seem to do much good. Dad reckons the baby's hungry. He says I should start him on solid food. A good dollop of porridge will set that nipper right, he says.'

'Richard is far too young for that, Daisy. Mother's milk is all he needs at such a young age. I do have one suggestion, though; try to keep him awake through the day. Then he may drop off at the proper time, even if he doesn't sleep all through as yet.'

Daisy sighed again. 'That's all very well, but where am I to find the time to attend to him all day long? If he starts bawling, Dad starts moaning, and they're driving me mad between the pair of them. And how long is my husband supposed to put up with finding me all at sixes and sevens when he comes in from work, expecting to find a good meal on the table?'

'I know it's hard for you at present,' Maudie told her, 'but that child will settle down eventually and you'll soon find your feet. Believe me, I know. Now, then, young Mrs Larke, we'll go in and face the dragon in his lair, shall we?' Daisy managed a weak giggle.

'And about time, too!' the dragon snorted, when Maudie set a strong cup of tea and a wedge of lardy cake in front of him.

'A word of thanks wouldn't go amiss,' Maudie told him.

'Thanks, is it? Ain't no more than my due! I don't know what's come over that girl of mine. Proper useless these days.'

'Oh, bite your tongue, do!' Maudie snapped, and to her surprise the old chap stopped moaning and began to slurp his tea. She wondered if she should have a word with Daisy's husband. If he could convince his father-in-law to stop riling the poor girl, tempers might improve all round.

As she wheeled her bicycle out of the gate, a thought occurred to Maudie. She didn't know whether the old chap was simply frustrated by pain and old age, or if he had always been bad-tempered. She could imagine him flaring up and landing a blow on somebody without thinking twice. She couldn't lay the blame on him for Swain's death, for as far as she knew he hadn't strayed beyond the doors since his arrival in Llandyfan, and in any case he was too feeble now.

The point was that the murderer might not have had any special motive for killing Swain. They might have disagreed over some matter totally unconnected with

Swain's reasons for coming to the area and come to blows as a result. Wait a minute, though, Maudie Rouse! Swain was strangled. It takes more than a flash of bad temper to garrote a man!

* * *

Back at the parish hall, Maudie was pleased to see Mrs Blunt waiting for her. 'I was meaning to come and see you,' she said, propping her machine against the wall of the building.

'Oh, yes? What about?'

'I've just come from the Larkes' cottage. Something needs to be done for that poor young Daisy. She's run off her feet looking after that miserable old codger of a father of hers as well as a new baby, and I wonder if the church can be of help.'

'What did you have in mind?'

'Are there perhaps some helpful grandmothers who might enjoy taking the baby off her hands now and then? Take him out for a walk in his pram, say?'

'That should be easy enough to

arrange,' Mrs Blunt said. 'And perhaps her father could benefit from some visits from our churchwardens. Oh, not to read him the riot act! No, indeed. Just a friendly visit to have a game of cards or something.'

'Just what the Nurse ordered,' Maudie said.

10

Maudie was about to leave her office for the day when a visitor arrived. Shrugging off her uniform coat again, she returned to her hard wooden chair, her dream of relaxing with her feet up receding fast. She was relieved when the new arrival turned out to be Emma Plummer, the infants' teacher at the village school. At least the young woman wouldn't be bringing news of an impending confinement; nor, judging by her calm demeanour, had there been an accident.

'Miss Rice sent me,' the girl began. 'She wants the nit nurse.'

Maudie assumed that the headmistress had no need of such a person for herself. 'Oh, yes? Is this just a routine check-up, then?'

The girl wrinkled her nose. 'Head lice! Ugh! I saw them myself, on a little boy in my class. His scalp was crawling with them, Nurse. I could hardly bear to look.'

'Children from the cleanest of homes can get them, Miss Plummer. Head lice can get passed on very quickly when children work in close quarters.'

'So I understand. Can I leave it with you, then, to contact the nit nurse?'

'Here in the country we don't have the resources to hire a nurse for that specific purpose, but yes, you can leave it with me. Nurse McGrath from Brookfield usually sees to these inspections, but she's on leave at the moment and I'm not sure if her replacement can be spared. I'll give her a call and see what can be done.'

'They'll have to have their heads shaved, I suppose,' the girl said. 'There was a boy at my last school like that. At least he wasn't a girl, having to lose long plaits.'

'I think you'll find that was to do with ringworm,' Maudie assured her. 'The treatment for head lice is much less drastic. Parents will be given a bottle of foul smelling liquid and a toothcomb and told to give nightly applications of the stuff. And I suggest that you give yourself a regular shampoo, just in case.'

The girl left, shuddering. Maudie repressed a grin. If the girl remained in the teaching profession she was likely to see worse sights than a few nits. She picked up the phone to call Brookfield.

'I'm so sorry,' Nurse O'Neill told her, 'But they'll just have to manage without me. I'm up to my eyebrows here and I don't see how I could get away, even for a day. I've got two babies with croup, a man with a broken ankle, two people with mysterious stomach cramps and a woman who keeps threatening to jump off the railway bridge and end it all. I'm going wild trying to go from one to the other, and your old Doc Mallory is no help. I've tried to get him to come out to look at some of them but all I can get out of him is 'I'm sure you can manage, Nurse.' Honestly, what's the point of having a doctor on tap if you can't get hold of him when he's needed? All he's good for is writing prescriptions or shipping people off to the cottage hospital.'

'He's getting up in years,' Maudie explained. 'He was dragged back out of retirement at the start of the war and never let go again. I daresay he was a good enough man in his day, but he's old and tired now. We all hope that when this new National Health scheme comes into place next year we'll get some younger men here, preferably one or two in each village.'

'I hope you're right. Meanwhile, I'm sorry, but I'm afraid you'll have to make other arrangements, because I can't come over to you just now.'

'I quite understand. I suppose I'll have to deal with it myself. What about the poor woman who's threatening to do away with herself? Has the doctor given her anything?'

'She has pills, yes, but she won't take them unless I'm standing over her while she swallows. What she really needs is a psychiatric assessment, but her husband doesn't want to spend the money. He says she's just a bit run down and she'll snap out of it in time.'

'Typical! Well, I mustn't keep you. Hot buttered teacakes are calling to me, louder by the minute.'

'Lucky for some,' Nurse O'Neill

laughed and hung up the phone.

'And that leaves me to deal with an outbreak of head lice,' Maudie moaned as she replaced the receiver none too gently in its place. This was definitely not what I signed on for when I took my midwifery training, she thought. But she was a nurse, first and last, and she knew she would turn up at the school and do the task she dreaded.

* * *

St John's was a Church of England school run by a board of governors. The early Victorian building had two rooms where the children of Llandyfan had been educated for generations. Maudie had once asked the vicar why his church was called St John's when their village was Llandyfan. She knew a few words of Welsh and believed that the name had something to do with a monk's cell.

The vicar was a keen local historian. 'Our village was founded, and probably named, by a wealthy Welshman named Parry who came here in the eighteenth century,' he explained. 'Dyfan was a saint of the Celtic Church. But of course St John's has been here for hundreds of years, at the centre of a very ancient parish. When the school was built it was of course, as a church institution, named after the church and not the village.'

The builders of the school certainly had some Victorian ideas, Maudie thought, looking at it now. The windows were set high enough in the walls that children seated at their desks would not be distracted by what was going on in the world outside. Even the doors bore witness to Victorian ideals; there was one entrance marked Girls and another for Boys.

A plump woman appeared at the latter door, vigorously ringing a hand bell. This was Miss Rice, the headmistress. Screaming children stopped their games and ran to her, forming lines as they came. 'No talking! Take your distance!' she bellowed, waiting while each child placed a hand on the shoulder of the one in front while taking a step backwards.

Maudie marvelled at the speed with which the woman brought the youngsters under control, marching them inside the school in an orderly fashion. She told herself that she could never manage a group of unruly children in so masterly a manner, which was probably why she had never considered school teaching as a choice of career. On the other hand, she was pretty sure that the efficient Miss Rice would never make a midwife. Or was that simply wishful thinking?

Having waited while the headmistress conducted prayers, Maudie made her way to the junior classroom where Miss Plummer's pupils awaited her ministrations.

'This is Nurse Rouse, who has come to examine your heads,' the young teacher announced. The children gazed at Maudie, some with fear in their eyes, others grinning. Most of them already knew her, of course. A boy raised his hand.

'Yes, Arnold?'

'Please, Miss, if we've got them nits, do we have to stay home till we're all better?'

Maudie shook her head. 'There's no need for that, my lad, so don't you get any ideas! Mummy will treat you at home, and we'll soon get rid of the nasty things.'

'Aw! It's not fair!'

'Life isn't fair, child. Now, then, arms on desks! Heads down!'

Well trained, the children rested their heads on their arms and Maudie moved into action 'Eyes closed, Arnold Rivers!' she snapped, and was gratified to see the little eyelids close. Perhaps she would have made a teacher after all!

After that she moved to the senior classroom, where the process was repeated. 'I'm afraid we've got almost one hundred per cent infestation,' she told the Head when her examination was complete and the children had been sent outside to play.

'I was afraid of that, Nurse. When we have them sitting four to a desk it's impossible to maintain any distance between them, and lice can hop. Well, I'll run off some notices on the Gestetner and they can take the good news home to Mummy.'

'Thank you, Miss Rice. I've put in a requisition for new typewriter ribbons, but they haven't arrived yet. The old one is so worn that I have to use the red side for everything. I'm afraid I wouldn't make a very good fist of preparing the master for the ditto machine.'

When she was leaving the school, carefully making her way through the throng of skipping girls, Maudie noticed one child standing apart from the others. Recognizing her as little Lily Willis, she was about to smile and move on when she sensed that the girl wanted to speak to her. Lily must have been among the pupils she had just examined, but they'd all kept their heads down and she hadn't taken note of their faces as she walked along the rows.

'Hello, Lily,' she said, smiling. 'Were you waiting to speak to me? Is there something you want to ask me?'

Lily looked down at her little wooden clogs. 'Mum says we mustn't talk to strangers,' she mumbled.

'And quite right, too. I'm not a stranger though, am I? I'm Nurse Rouse, and I've been to your home, haven't I? If something is worrying you, you can tell me, Lily, and I may be able to help. That's what nurses do.' The child looked up at her then.

'*She* talked to a stranger,' she said, nodding as if to underline her point.

'Who did? Was it Mummy?'

Maudie was never to hear the answer because at that moment a small body detached itself from the little knot of skipping girls, madly hurtling its way towards them and delivering a sharp kick to Lily's shin. Enraged, the child pushed her attacker to the ground and sped away.

'Polly Willis! Whatever made you do a thing like that?'

Either the little girl had not yet found her tongue, or she was too upset to respond. Scrambling to her feet, she ran off to join her friends, and Maudie was left standing with her mouth open.

11

'It was all rather peculiar,' Maudie told Mrs Blunt later that day. 'I'm sure there was something she wanted to confide in me, but she couldn't quite get it out. Then Polly came and interrupted us, as if she wanted to prevent Lily from talking. You've had children of your own. What do you make of it all?'

Mrs Blunt shrugged. 'You know children. They tend to get funny little ideas in their heads. Very often it doesn't mean much. They chew on something for a while and then they get hold of some new notion and they run with that.'

'But it seemed to me that Lily was anxious because her mum had warned her not to talk to strangers.'

'Every mother worth her salt tells her children that, Nurse.'

'Of course, but could there be more to it in this case?'

'Having to do with Polly's disappearance, do you mean? I wouldn't be surprised. After all, nobody knows what became of the child during those hours when she was missing, and Mrs Willis suffered a terrible shock. I'm sure the poor woman has kept those little girls on a tight rein ever since, giving them all sorts of threats and warnings. The trouble is that we grown-ups know all too well what can happen to innocent little girls, yet how do you get that across to them without scaring them out of their wits, or telling them things they can't possibly understand?'

* * *

The next afternoon Maudie cycled to an outlying farm to make an antenatal visit to a teenaged mother-to-be who lived with her disapproving parents. The girl's condition was euphemistically referred to as being 'in trouble' and although she was perfectly healthy and could have been brought into the village to consult the midwife, her parents wanted to keep her hidden.

'Not that it's any secret,' the prospective grandmother muttered. 'Them village gossips will have broadcasted it all over the county by now. I knew it was a mistake to let Greta go to them village hops! The vicar ought to get them stopped, that's what I say. I'll never be able to hold my head up in public after this, Nurse. I've had to stop going to the W.I. on account of them old tabbies looking at me sideways, like I don't know how to bring up my daughter in the fear of the Lord. I don't know how I'll ever be able to bear the disgrace.'

'It's not as bad as all that, Mrs Black. Greta isn't the first girl to get into this pickle, and I don't suppose she'll be the last. As long as mother and baby come through this safely, that's all that really matters, and I'm here to see that they do.'

'And Matt and me's going to get wed,' Greta said, tossing her auburn curls.

'Huh! I'll believe that when I see it!' her mother snapped.

'Can we go somewhere for you to lie down?' Maudie asked. 'I want to have a look at you, Greta, and ask you a few questions. This is just routine.'

'I'll take you up to her room,' Mrs Black said, 'although whether it's fit to be seen is another question. If you ever do get wed, my girl, you'll have to buck up your ideas in a hurry, and that's a fact.'

'I think we can manage, Mrs Black,' Maudie said firmly. 'I'd prefer to see Greta alone, if you don't mind.'

For a long moment it seemed as if the woman was about to protest, but then her hands fell to her sides and she backed away, as if retreating from a dog of uncertain temper. 'Do what you must, Nurse. I'll be down here if you need me.'

Maudie followed the girl up the uncarpeted stairs and into a chilly bedroom which, as Mrs Black had feared, was desperately untidy. Clothing was strewn everywhere and the bed was just as Greta must have left it when she'd got up that morning. The walls were covered with so many pictures of film stars, torn from magazines, that Maudie could barely make out the rose-patterned wallpaper.

'Do you like my pictures, Nurse?' Greta

gazed adoringly at the array of faces. She pointed to one that held pride of place over the head of the bed. 'See her? That's Greta Garbo, that is. I'm called after her. When my mum was expecting me she went to see one of her films. *Anna Christie*, it was called. Mum thought Greta was ever such a lovely name, so she gave it to me.

'And that there's Veronica Lake,' she went on, pointing again. 'I'm going to do my hair like hers as soon as it grows long enough. And what do you think of Tyrone Power? I could really go for him. It must be wonderful in Hollywood. Did you ever wish you could go there, Nurse?'

'Not particularly. I've too much work to do here to go gadding off to America. Now, let's get you lying down, shall we, while I have a look at your tummy?'

Soon afterwards Maudie was on her way home, reflecting that there would never be any shortage of work for those in her profession. Now that the war was over there would be a boom in the birth rate as servicemen returned to their wives and families and life began to return to normal. At the same time, there would always be the results of hasty couplings between youngsters such as Greta and Matt, for nature had arranged matters so that the planet would continue to be peopled.

She sighed. Despite Mrs Black's misgivings, it wasn't the thought of babies born out of wedlock that bothered her. She was far more concerned about married women who bore one child after another, to the detriment of their health. Her own grandmother had given birth to fourteen children — fifteen if you counted that miscarriage, discussed in whispers by the old aunts — and she was by no means unique. If only there was some reliable way to stop those pregnancies occurring, other than abstinence, which hardly appealed to most men, who demanded their 'rights.'

As she neared the cottage where the Willis family lived, she observed a child swinging on the gate. At that distance it was hard to tell which of the girls it was, for they not only looked alike but their mother dressed them in similar clothing so they might well be mistaken for twins. As she drew closer, Maudie felt sure that the child was Lily; of Polly there was no sign.

Her instinct told her that there was more to her little encounter with the child than Mrs Blunt had suggested. On impulse she braked, calling out to the girl. Lily approached slowly, glancing back at the house as she came.

'It's all right, dear. I just want a quick word. I shan't keep you long.'

She noticed that the child was staring in fascination at her black bag that was crammed into the basket in front of the bicycle.

'Is that the bag you bring the babies in, Nurse?'

Maudie smiled. 'Yes, that's right.'

'Why don't they get stuff-cated?'

'Do you mean suffocated, dear?'

'When we found caterpillars to take to school Daddy made holes in the top of the jar so they could breathe. So how can the babies breathe in that bag?'

'Oh, well,' Maudie said, improvising wildly, 'babies don't start to breathe until they are born, Lily. That is, after they come out of the bag, you see?'

'Oh. Ethel Parker's granny tells lies, she does! She says when Ethel was born they found her in the cabbage patch. That's silly!'

Maudie could feel a headache coming on. 'Babies come in different ways, Lily. In some countries a bird called a stork brings them. They fly over the rooftops until they find a house where somebody wants a baby and they take it in through the window.'

'Oo! I hope they don't drop any, then,' Lily said, wide-eyed. 'We want a baby at our house but I hope it doesn't come all squashed.'

Was it possible that Helen Willis was pregnant at last? If she was, she certainly hadn't notified Maudie. 'When the time comes for your Mum to get a new baby, I'll be bringing it in my bag, same as usual, so there's no need to worry. You'd like a new baby, would you, Lily?'

'Only if it's a boy,' the child said. 'You've got to promise you'll bring a boy, Nurse!'

There seems to be more here than meets the eye, Maudie thought. 'I'm sorry, Lily; that's the one thing I can't promise. We can't choose, you see.'

'But Dad says it must be a boy, Nurse. There's too many girls round here already, he says. He gets cross about it sometimes, and he makes Mum cry.'

Maudie gave no response to this as she mounted her bicycle and headed towards home. It sounded as if there might be some form of abuse going on at the Willis house, but what could she do about it? It was difficult to know what to do in such a case. It was not her place to interfere between husband and wife, and indeed any such intervention could make matters worse for the victim. But what if the man was unkind, or worse, to his two little girls? Could that be what had caused Polly's disappearance, and might it not account for her silence now?

She considered her options. Mrs Blunt was a sensible woman; she could discuss her suspicions with the vicar's wife without fearing that the matter would go any further. But by doing so, would

Maudie label Bob Willis unfairly as a wife-beater? How much credence could she place on young Lily's prattling? The best of children could test a parent's patience at times, causing them to flare up momentarily; why should she read more into the man's offhand comment than there really was?

But on the other hand, how would she feel if something bad happened and she had failed to prevent it? You're a midwife, Maudie Rouse, not a social worker, she admonished herself, but somehow the feeling of something bad waiting to happen would not go away.

12

'Good morning!' Mrs Blunt hailed Maudie as she approached the village shop. 'You're just in time, Nurse. Mrs Hatch has received a shipment of Garibaldi biscuits if you're interested. There's been quite a run on them this morning but you could be in luck if you get in there quickly.'

Maudie wrinkled her nose. 'I don't think so, thank you all the same. I'm not too keen on them, actually; they never seem to have much taste to them. Bourbons, now, I could eat a whole packet of those at one sitting. I think I'll hang on to my coupons until Mrs Hatch gets some of those.'

Maudie was a favourite with Mrs Hatch ever since she had treated her sprained wrist, thereby saving her an expensive visit to the doctor. The woman would kindly set aside some of the nurse's favourite treats if she ever did get hold of some, and she'd gladly tip her the wink. To the intense irritation of most British people food was still rationed, never mind the fact that the beastly war had been over for two years. Only this year potatoes had actually been put on the list, which was a real shocker, although here in the countryside it did not have much effect because most people grew their own.

Maudie had no time for gardening, but she could always rely on her patients to slip her a pound or two. In fact, some people paid her in kind. She had fond memories of the time when she'd been given a chicken, ready for the pot, after assisting a fine baby boy into the world. As for accepting the items Mrs Hatch put aside for her, Maudie had no qualms about that. Buying things 'under the counter', as it was known, was frowned upon, but neither woman thought of saving those biscuits as dealing on the black market. If when it came to it Maudie had used up all the current points in her ration book, that would be that; the cherished Bourbons would go to some other customer. Maudie worked unsociable hours as it was and she had no time to waste queuing for biscuits.

'I see the flags are flying for Phyllis Dempster,' Mrs Blunt said, tearing open the packet of Garibaldis with her teeth. 'Are you sure you won't have one of these, Nurse?'

Maudie's mouth watered at the thought of food but she shook her head. 'That's right. I warned her last week that it was time she got busy, so I'm glad to see that she paid attention to me. There's nothing worse than having the baby arrive without things ready to receive it.'

The sight of nappies drying on the line at a house where there had previously been no baby was a sign to the community that the situation was about to change. 'Of course, she's an old hand at this,' Maudie went on. 'She does have older children. The youngest little boy is five now, almost ready to start school.'

'She won't be needing the Box, then,' the vicar's wife said. 'She'll have a good stock of garments left over from the older children. It's just as well, for the nappies are getting past it. The towelling ones are not too bad, but the muslin ones have seen better days.'

The Box, as it was known locally, was the result of a custom left over from Victorian times, when enormous families were the norm and money was scarce. Baby supplies were kept at the vicarage, available for borrowing by the poor women of the village. When the baby was too old to need them, the garments would be carefully laundered and returned to the vicarage with sprigs of lavender laid between the folds. Having fallen into abeyance in the more prosperous times between the wars, it had been brought back into use when clothing and fabrics had been rationed by the government. With a bit of scrimping and saving most people could afford to clothe their children now, but if they spent all their coupons on nappies and baby nighties that would leave none to clothe the rest of the family.

'Speaking of the Box,' Maudie said, 'I've had an idea. What about a nappy drive? There must be plenty of women hereabouts whose families are complete.

Why shouldn't they donate their left over baby things?'

'It sounds like a good idea,' Mrs Blunt said, 'but you know how superstitious people can be. They believe that as soon as they give their baby things away, they'll find they're expecting again.'

'Excuse me, Nurse, can I have a word?' Hand over her heart, Maudie swung around to find Phyllis Dempster behind her.

'Mrs Dempster! I didn't hear you coming. What can I do for you?'

'I don't want to interrupt . . . '

Mrs Blunt took the hint. 'I must be running along,' she said, smiling at the newcomer. 'How are you, Mrs Dempster?'

'Fair to middling, ta. Nurse, would you mind coming over to the house? The thing is, I've left our Bobby alone, and goodness knows what he'll get up to while my back is turned.'

Nothing more was said until the pair were sitting in the Dempsters' cramped little kitchen, with Bobby at their feet, making *vroom-vroom* noises as he played with a battered toy car.

'There's measles over at Midvale,' the young mother said, biting her lip. 'My cousin and her little girl came to visit last week, and now I hear that her Angela has it. I'm that worried, Nurse, that it may harm this one.' She patted her swollen abdomen. 'And what if my two come down with it? Won't that make it worse?'

Maudie smiled. 'I believe it's the red measles they have over there, and it may well come here. And yes, there's a possibility that your two may catch it, and very unpleasant it can be, too. But it's German measles that can harm a baby in the womb, and that's a quite different disease. Besides, you're so far along with your pregnancy that there's no fear of complications of that sort.'

'Are you sure, Nurse?'

'As sure as I can be,' Maudie assured her, wondering why the woman continued to frown. 'I'll just check your blood pressure while I'm here,' she said, opening her bag. Young Bobby watched her, wide-eyed, as she fitted the cuff around her patient's upper arm.

'What's that thing for, Nurse?'

'It's called a sphygmomanometer,' she told him. 'Can you say that?'

The little boy shook his head. 'No, I didn't think so. And this is called a stethoscope. I'm going to listen to Mummy's heart beating. Shall I listen to yours as well?'

'No! Don't want it!' Maudie grinned at him, but her smile faded when she heard the relentless thumping of his mother's heart, and noted the reading that was well above normal. 'Your BP is up a little,' she murmured. 'Just let me feel your ankles, if you don't mind.'

But her patient's ankles, although chafed from going without stockings, felt normal enough. There were no symptoms of possible toxaemia.

'Is something else worrying you, Mrs Dempster? You're getting sufficient rest, are you?'

The woman shrugged. 'As much as anyone can, running around after this lot. That man's been round here again, that's all. I suppose I'm stupid to let it worry me, but there's something about him I don't quite cotton on to.'

'What man?'

'Oh, just a chap who knocked on the door one day a few weeks back. Looking for lodgings, just for a few nights, he said. We've no spare room here, I told him, so he went off down the street and I never saw him again until the day before yesterday. Mind you, I thought it was odd when he never knocked at any of the other doors. I saw him looking at our Rosie and I didn't care for that at all. There's some funny types about, and I don't mean funny-ha-ha. Then little Polly Willis went missing and I started to wonder.'

'Did you report this to the police?'

'My Harry had a word with Dick Bryant in the pub, and he said they'd look into it. We never heard no more about it, and then Polly came home, walking into her house as bold as brass, so I put it out of my mind until he turned up again.'

'He came to your door?'

'No, no. He was in the phone box at the crossroads. The other evening I thought I'd give our Sandra a ring to see how little Angela was, her with the measles; and when I got there, that's when I saw the chap.'

'What does he look like? I'll keep an eye open for him when I'm making my rounds.'

'Oh, nothing special,' Mrs Dempster said. 'Medium height, dark hair, a bit of a paunch. Chaps like him are ten-a-penny.'

'And about how old, would you say?'

'Late thirties, early forties.'

'Any distinguishing marks?'

Mrs Dempster summoned up a giggle at last. 'No scars or wooden legs, Nurse. Nothing that would make him stand out in a crowd. And his clothes was ordinary, too. A pinstriped suit that didn't fit too well. I reckon it was one of them demob suits they give them. You know, when they get let out of the army. Oh, and his shirt collar was frayed at the edges. I took special note of that because I've had to turn Harry's collars for him. Can't have him going to work in shirts that are only fit for the rag and bone man.'

Maudie mulled this information over in her mind as she walked back to her cottage. It was only when she went to light the gas to cook her evening meal that she realized she'd forgotten to buy the matches she'd gone to the shop for. Muttering, she settled for cold baked beans eaten directly out of the tin. There was no point in making unnecessary work for herself.

13

Maudie sat in the Copper Kettle, rather pleased with herself and with the way her day was working out. She had arranged her home visits to women who lived in outlying areas so that she was back in the village by noon. She could enjoy a leisurely lunch before setting off in the opposite direction. There was no point in turning up at peoples' homes when they were trying to dish up their own meals. She preferred to sit down with her patients for a quiet chat. Half the battle in her business was convincing her mothers that they were in safe hands. Stress did nobody any good. This was especially true with a woman who was approaching a first confinement, having no idea of what to expect.

Maudie often wondered why women were always so ready to regale others with horror stories and old wives' tales.

Perhaps it had something to do with a sort of maternal snobbery. 'I had to suffer, so why shouldn't everyone else have to suffer too?'

'What'll it be, Nurse?' Maudie came to with a start, realizing that the elderly waitress was waiting to take her order.

'Oh, hello, Mary. How are your bunions these days?'

'Fair to middling, Nurse. Mustn't grumble. Now, then, I've got some lovely chocolate eclairs, or I can cut you a slice of Battenberg if you like.'

'Eclairs,' Maudie sighed. 'I'd better not. They'll go straight to my hips. I'll have cheese on toast, please, and a bowl of your mulligatawny soup.'

'Right you are. Won't be two ticks.'

Leaning back in her chair, Maudie observed a young woman entering the tearoom. Her swagger coat was hanging open and Maudie surveyed her swollen abdomen with a professional eye. 'Five months gone, by the look of it,' she mouthed silently.

'Who is that person sitting at the table for two?' she asked, when the waitress had placed a bowl of steaming soup in front of her.

'Oh, her. She's married to a labouring chap who does road repairs for the council. They haven't been here long. I think they've rented that tumbledown cottage that used to belong to old man Fowler, him that died last year. Mind you, I say belong, though he only rented the place, same as them now. Owning houses isn't for people like us.'

Another patient for me, then, Maudie thought as she attacked her meal. I wonder why she hasn't been to see me before now? Maudie had enough to do without soliciting patients, but on the other hand it was important that pregnant women had good antenatal care. Part of Maudie's job was to assess women to gauge whether a home birth was right for them. Childbirth was a natural process and few of her patients would have dreamed of choosing to deliver their babies in a hospital setting, but on occasion it was the only safe option.

The girl was still lingering over her snack when Maudie got up to leave. She held a half-eaten cream bun in one hand and her lips were smeared with ersatz cream. A second bun awaited her attention on its blue willow pattern plate.

Maudie paused. 'Hello! Let me introduce myself. I'm Nurse Rouse, the midwife for this district.'

The girl looked at her with myopic blue eyes. 'Oh, yeah?' she mumbled through a mouthful of bun.

'I understand you're new here,' Maudie said, pulling out a chair and sliding into it. 'Only you haven't registered with me yet so I thought you might like to do that soon.'

'What for?' the girl demanded, cramming the remains of the bun into her mouth.

'Well, proper care is essential to the health of mother and baby. And I can give you advice on the various aspects of pregnancy.' Such as proper diet, Maudie thought, watching in fascination as the girl picked up the remaining bun and took an enormous bite. 'So why don't we set up an appointment now?' she asked. 'You can see me at my office, or I'd be glad to make a home visit. What do you say, Mrs er . . . ?'

'Patsy Sawyer is my name, and I don't need no midwife.'

'You might change your mind about that when your time comes,' Maudie said grimly.

'No, I won't. My gran will bring the baby, same as she always does in our family.'

'Is she a trained midwife, then?'

'Well, she may not be one of you lot, but she knows what she's doing. My mum's had seven kids, see, and Gran saw to the lot of them.'

Maudie nodded. Since the beginning of time women in labour had been attended by knowledgeable local women or family members, often to the satisfaction of all concerned. Just as often something went wrong, either at the time of birth or later as a result of complications. Employing a trained midwife greatly reduced the mortality rate, not least because she knew when it was necessary to summon the doctor or to send a woman to hospital.

'Why not come to see me anyway, just

to make sure?' she said gently. She made a quick calculation in her head. 'Let's see now; when do you expect Baby? In December, perhaps?'

Patsy shook her head, sending a spray of crumbs over the table. 'End of February, Gran says.'

And you'll be lucky to get past Christmas, Maudie thought, but she said nothing as she stood up to leave. She only hoped that the wonderful Gran would be on hand when the baby made its surprise appearance, otherwise it would be Maudie Rouse who was called on to pick up the pieces. She sighed. Part of the reason that good healthcare was so lacking in country places was that people were unwilling, or unable, to pay the fees involved. She hoped that might change when the National Health Service started up in 1948, but she would have to wait and see.

* * *

As she wheeled her bicycle past the Royal Oak she noticed a man opening the side door that gave access to the upper rooms. Len Frost occasionally put up overnight guests there, mostly tourists who were passing through. There was no money in it, he told anyone who would listen, but at least if they had a bed to go to you could encourage them to drink up, without fear of them coming to grief on the roads.

At that distance Maudie could not see the man's face, which was half obscured by a trilby hat. What she did notice was the navy blue pinstriped suit he was wearing, with heavily padded shoulders. On impulse she propped her machine against the wall of the pub and hurried inside. The landlord, busily polishing glasses with a skill born of long practice, greeted her amiably.

'If it's your dinner you're wanting, Nurse, you've had it. We stopped serving ten minute ago. I s'pose I could do you a cheese sandwich though, if you're desperate. Mustn't have you fainting on the job and collapsing on top of some poor woman in the family way, must we?' He guffawed at his own wit.

'That's all right, Len, thanks all the

same. I've just come from the Copper Kettle. I wanted to ask you about a chap I've jut seen going in the side door. Who is he?'

'Him? Oh, that'll be John Smith, from up London way.'

'Smith, eh? That seems fishy to me. It makes me think he's got something to hide.'

'You've no call to think that, Nurse. There's thousands in the world by that name and most of them honest as the day, most likely.'

'But what's he doing in Llandyfan, then? He's not exactly dressed for rambling or bird watching.'

'He's a travelling salesman. A rep for some company up London, he says.'

'What sort of company? Have you seen his case of samples?'

The landlord regarded Maudie with his head to one side. 'You've got a proper old bee in your bonnet, Nurse. He's just some poor chap trying to make a living any way he can. There's a lot of that about, you know, men coming back from the war with no jobs to go to. The government ought to do something for them, poor devils.'

'You could be right, Len,' Maudie admitted, 'but I think he bears looking into. As for me having a bee in my bonnet, as you put it. Don't forget that it was me who found the body of poor old Swain. I'll never forget that, not until my dying day, so you can't blame me for being suspicious of strangers.'

'Right you are, Nurse,' the landlord told her.

14

Maudie returned to Llandyfan after a satisfactory day at Brookfield, where she had met with three expectant mothers at the health office there. Only one of the women was nearing her delivery date, and Maudie gave her explicit instructions concerning what to do when the time came.

'You're to get hold of Nurse O'Neill when you go into labour, and she will decide whether to send for me, all right?'

'Yes, Nurse, but shouldn't we phone you directly, to make sure you get here in time?'

'There's such a thing as false labour, Mrs Coombs. Little practice runs for the birth process, if I may put it like that. I don't want to come galloping over here only to find that you're still some days away from delivery. And don't you worry; you'll be quite safe with Nurse O'Neill.'

When the women had left, Maudie

turned to Mairead. 'It's a bit of a nuisance, me being so far away, but I'm sure you'll be able to manage until I get here. This is her first pregnancy so we can expect a fairly long labour, of course. Give me a call as soon as labour is under way and I'll come at once. If there's no bus due I'll come by taxi.'

'Won't that cost a lot, all the way from Llandyfan?'

'Yes, but the safety of mother and baby is more important than money, as I'm sure Mr Coombs will agree. And if anyone thinks I'm going to cycle ten miles to attend a case, they've got another thing coming!'

Maudie was joking, of course. She would have crawled over hot coals to reach one of her patients in labour, if the need arose. 'And you must call Doc Mallory if any complications arise, or if — heaven forbid — something prevents me from coming. I should be all right, though; none of my local mums are due around that time.'

* * *

When Maudie reached her own office she sat down at her desk, still wearing her coat and hat, and carefully made up her case notes. Having locked away her filing cabinet she stood up to leave, looking forward to spending a leisurely evening at home, followed by an early night. She had a number of home visits planned for the next day that involved cycling to the furthest corners of her district.

As she wrenched open the door she almost collided with the vicar's wife, who had her hand on the outside knob. 'Oh, sorry! I didn't hear you coming. Are you all right?'

'Oh, I'm all right,' Mrs Blunt said, 'which is more than you can say for poor Miss Plummer.'

'Why, what do you mean? She hasn't had an accident, has she?'

'You haven't heard, then. She's been attacked. Somebody tried to strangle her last night.'

'No!'

'I'm afraid so. I did think you'd have heard. It must be all over the village by now.'

'I was off first thing. I caught the early bus to Brookfield. I had to help Nurse O'Neill with a couple of home visits, and then there was an antenatal clinic. Is the poor girl all right? Do they know who did it?'

'Apparently the police are interviewing someone. Helping the police with their inquiries, isn't that what it's called?'

'Is it anyone we know?'

'According to the milkman it's that young chap that's been working as a caretaker at the school.'

'Well, if anyone knows anything, I suppose it would be Fred Woolton. He calls on just about everyone in the district.'

'Fred reckons the chap must have made advances to Miss Plummer, as he puts it, was spurned by her and then got angry and tried to throttle her. It has been known to happen, you know. Oh, I don't mean with the caretaker chappie, Nurse. I'm just talking in general.'

'I must go and see if the girl is all right,' Maudie said. 'Where is she, do you know?'

'At home I expect. Mrs Flyte is her landlady. Miss Plummer has a bedsitter there. Hawthorn Tree Cottage, down by the bridge.'

* * *

Maudie found the young teacher sitting on a sagging couch in Mrs Flyte's kitchen, with a plaid rug over her knees. The landlady greeted her with evident relief. 'Thank goodness you've come, Nurse! I did think we should have had the doctor, but the child didn't want to spend the money. I've put one of my Bert's old socks round her neck, with a good dollop of liniment, and that should do the trick.'

'I'll just take a look, shall I, Miss Plummer?' Maudie carefully removed the hairy grey sock, wincing as the pungent smell of horse liniment reached her nostrils.

'Emma. My name's Emma,' the girl croaked.

'The area looks red and inflamed but the skin isn't broken,' Maudie observed, replacing the sock. The locals set great store by an old sock round the neck in cases of stiffness, though why a new sock or scarf wouldn't do just as well she couldn't think. Still, these old folk beliefs often worked well, simply because people had faith in them. It looked as if the girl had been lucky.

'What exactly happened?' she asked.

'Oh, she don't want to think about that!' Mrs Flyte muttered, red in the face with indignation. 'That Dick Bryant's already been here, asking this and that. Best to forget all about it now, that's what I say.'

'It may do her good to talk about it,' Maudie said. 'It never does any good to bottle things up inside, and I know that for a fact. I was dreaming about that poor man I found for weeks afterwards.'

'That's where it happened,' the girl whispered.

'What?' Maudie pulled up a wooden chair and sank down on it, all ears.

'Up there on the hill, where you found the body. That's where he got me. If those Cubs hadn't come running past I'd be lying there dead now.' She burst into tears, gasping and sobbing.

'There, now! Just see what you've done!' Mrs Flyte bent over and swept the girl into her arms, glaring at Maudie.

'It's all right, Mrs Flyte, I do want to talk about it,' Emma gasped, wriggling free. 'Do you think you could make me a cup of tea, please? It might soothe my throat.'

'And put plenty of sugar in it, too,' Maudie ordered. 'It's good for shock, and do the same for yourself, Mrs Flyte. Now then, my girl, just what were you doing up there on the hill, and at night, too?'

'It wasn't dark, Nurse. I'd been to visit one of my pupils who is in bed with a cold. I took him some books from the school library. He's getting on so well with his reading and I thought it would give him something to do while he's cooped up at home. He asked me to tell him a story, so I did, and I stayed longer than I meant to. I had lessons to prepare and that's why I decided to take the short cut back past the Bassett farm. It was only dusk and I thought I'd be all right.' She gulped. 'I mean, everyone says that whoever killed that poor man must be far away by now, so I thought I'd be safe if I hurried.'

'And then?' Maudie prompted, ignoring the look of outrage on Mrs Flyte's grim features.

'And then there was a sort of rustling in the bushes, and somebody grabbed me from behind. I struggled but he was too strong for me, and I sort of collapsed to the ground. Then all these little boys rushed into the clearing, jostling and shouting, and I suppose that frightened the man off.' She fingered her neck. 'There were two leaders with them and they made a bandy chair to carry me down to the farm. The police were called, and I told Constable Bryant what I could, which wasn't much. He says that perhaps Simon is to blame, but that's just ridiculous. Simon wouldn't hurt a flea.'

Maudie longed to ask more, but her trained eye told her that Emma Plummer was at the end of her tether. 'It's bed for you, my girl,' she said firmly. 'Can you help me get her upstairs, Mrs Flyte? I'll come back and see how you are tomorrow, Emma. Meanwhile, it's a couple of Aspros and a good night's rest for you.'

15

Maudie reached her cottage to find the vicar's wife waiting on the doorstep, clutching a posy of flowers.

'How is she?' Mrs Blunt asked. 'I saw you coming so I dashed round with these. I assume you'll be seeing Miss Plummer tomorrow, so do take her these, with my love. If you leave them in water overnight they should be all right.'

'I've made her take a couple of aspirins and I've put her to bed. Physically there's no lasting damage that I can see; the Wolf Cub pack turned up in the nick of time. Mentally, I'm not so sure. Even though she realizes she could have ended up dead, I don't think it's really sunk in yet.' Maudie shuddered. Her own nasty experience still loomed large in her mind.

'What do the police think? Are they still interrogating Simon whatsisname?'

'Don't ask me. Emma insists that he couldn't possibly have been responsible for the attack on her, but I need to know more before I can venture an opinion. Perhaps she'll be more forthcoming tomorrow. What do you know about the chap?'

Mrs Blunt spread her hands wide. 'I can't say that I've ever met him, but my Harold knows him and seems to approve.'

'He's not local, is he, this Simon?'

'Birmingham originally, I think,' Mrs Blunt said.

'Then what's he doing working as a caretaker in a place like this?' Maudie wondered.

'According to Harold he was a school teacher before the war, somewhere in Warwickshire, I believe. Then he got called up and spent the next few years in the army. When he came back to civvy street he couldn't get a teaching job for love nor money, so he had to take what he could get. He came to these parts on some sort of bird watching holiday, just at the time when old Saul Meadows had his heart attack and had to give up as janitor of the school here.'

'I remember that,' Maudie said. 'Saul

having his heart attack, I mean. I had no idea who took his place, though, not that I gave it any thought. It must have been a bit of a comedown for this Simon if he was a qualified school teacher.'

Mrs Blunt shrugged. 'Any port in a storm, I suppose. At least it shows he's not afraid to tackle honest work. Perhaps he thought it might help, being on the spot if a vacancy happened to come up on the staff that he might step into. Well, I must go and get Harold's tea. There's a vestry meeting tonight and he won't want to be late. Take these flowers, then, and I'll let you get on.'

Maudie accepted the little bouquet, admiring the purple and yellow pansies ringed about with sprigs of gypsophilia. She pressed the flowers to her nose but there was very little scent to them. Give her a nice bunch of lavender any day!

She wondered why this Simon had come under suspicion, if indeed there was any truth to the story that the police had taken him in. Probably some villager had fingered him as the only possibility because he was an incomer. Who among them would dream of assaulting an innocent young schoolteacher? It could only be a stranger who would do that; never one of their own!

If Emma was up to talking in the morning, Maudie decided, she would put a few tactful questions to her. What was the girl's relationship with Simon? Had he asked her out? Had he given her any indication that he could turn violent if thwarted in any way?

* * *

Emma Plummer was fully dressed and sitting in a bedside armchair when Maudie arrived bright and early the next morning. Smiling, Maudie handed her the posy and relayed the message of goodwill sent by the vicar's wife.

'I'm surprised to see you up and about already,' she said. 'I should have thought you'd want a lie-in this morning.'

'Constable Bryant sent a message to say he'll call in this morning to have a chat about what happened. I didn't want to do that in my pyjamas, Nurse. Besides, now I've washed my face and done my hair I feel more like facing the world.'

'And I'm going to do her a nice boiled egg with hot buttered soldiers,' Mrs Flyte said, smiling benignly at her lodger. Maudie could see that Emma had a gas ring which she could use to cook simple meals for herself after putting a shilling in the meter, but it was nice of the landlady to come up trumps with some comfort food.

'Have you heard anything about poor Simon?' Emma asked, when the older woman had left the room. 'They don't have him locked up, do they?'

'I really can't say, but I daresay Dick Bryant will let you know what's happening when he comes. Does this Simon have a last name?'

'Cox. His name is Simon Cox.'

'I see. And I understand that he's a teacher by profession, but filling in the time as caretaker while he hunts for a job in his own field?'

'That's right.'

'And how well do you know him?'

Emma blushed. 'We've been to the

pictures in Midvale a couple of times.'

'A nice chap, is he?'

'He's all right. Not really my type, but there aren't many single chaps of my age round here so we've sort of become friends.'

'And how does Mr Simon Cox feel about that? Perhaps he'd like it to be something more?'

'If you think he tried to kill me because I've turned him down or something, you couldn't be more wrong!' Emma cried. 'As I said, we're just friends, that's all. Simon was engaged to a girl before the war but he was away from England for such a long time that it sort of petered out. She left him high and dry in the end and married somebody else. Aside from that, he's decided he doesn't want to get involved in another relationship at the moment. He thinks he has nothing to offer a girl now. He has that part-time job at the school and that barely covers the cost of the boarding house where he stays.'

Maudie's ears pricked up. 'Boarding house? You don't mean Mrs Logan's, by any chance?'

'Who?'

'Mrs Logan over at Brookfield.'

Emma shook her head. 'Simon doesn't own a car. He couldn't afford to run one, and he couldn't very well cycle or walk ten miles each way to get to work.'

'That would be difficult,' Maudie admitted. She had done it herself once or twice, but she wouldn't want to take it on every day. 'Oh, well, it was just a thought. Mrs Logan was Cyril Swain's landlady. I wondered if there was some connection between his death and the attack on you. After all, they both happened in the same place.'

Emma swallowed hard. 'You don't really think so, do you? I didn't know Mr Swain, or anything about him. Unless some maniac is going around killing anybody who goes up on that hill, why would he want to kill me?'

'Why, indeed?'

Before the pair could say anything more there was a rap on the door, followed by the sound of low voices.

'That sounds like Dick Bryant,' Maudie said. 'Would you like me to stay with you, dear? If you find the interview too upsetting I could ask him to come back another time.'

But Dick Bryant was one of those old-fashioned policemen that children and old ladies instinctively trusted, the sort that parents advised their children to turn to in times of trouble. His ruddy complexion spoke of days spent in the open air, and the calm expression in his brown eyes made Maudie think of a particularly friendly dog.

'Is it safe to come in, Miss?'

'What's happened to Simon?' Emma cried, as soon as the constable put his head around the door. 'What have you done to him?'

'He's fine. We've let him go, without a stain on his character.'

'Have you? You must believe he didn't do it, then.'

'Mr Cox has an alibi. We've checked it out and he was miles away yesterday evening. He'd gone to Midvale to meet up with an old pal from army days. They attended a matinee performance of a film they wanted to see and went out for a meal afterwards. He returned by the evening bus, which as you know, doesn't get into Llandyfan until a quarter to ten. By that time your ordeal was over and you'd been brought back here. I assume you were safely tucked up in bed by then.'

'Indeed she was,' Maudie said. 'I put her there myself.'

'So that brings us to my next question, Miss. Who did attack you, and why?'

'Didn't those Cubs see anything?' Maudie wondered. 'Aren't Boy Scouts supposed to be observant?'

'They've been questioned, of course, and they're all agog to think they might be part of a real mystery, but it seems they appeared on the scene too late. As for their leaders, they were too busy trying to help you, Miss Plummer, to go crashing about in the shrubbery.'

'I think I must just have been in the wrong place at the wrong time,' Emma remarked. 'I'm an ordinary little schoolmistress in a Church of England school. As far as I know I haven't upset anybody and I don't even know any violent people.'

'There's something you should know,

Jim,' Maudie said suddenly. 'There's a chap staying at the Royal Oak at the moment. According to Len Frost he's some sort of sales rep.'

'Nothing odd about that, Nurse. Reps have always stayed there. That's why Len keeps those rooms, to make a bit extra on the side.'

'Ah, but this fellow was in the district when poor old Swain was killed.'

'What's that?'

Maudie told her story. 'He looks like a spiv to me,' she concluded. 'He wears a pinstriped suit with big shoulder pads. Not the sort of thing you usually find hereabouts. He has a thin face with a beaky sort of nose, and dark hair, smarmed down with Brylcreem.'

'I have seen a man like that,' Emma said slowly, 'hanging around the school on a couple of occasions. I saw him when I was outside on playground duty.'

Bryant was immediately on the alert. 'What was he doing? Did he say anything?'

'He was talking to one of the boys through the railings. I was about to go and say something when a child fell over and grazed her knee, and I had to see to her. When I looked up again he'd gone.'

Bryant exchanged glances with Maudie. 'I'll need to have a word with that boy,' he said grimly. 'Think back, please. Can you recall who he was?'

16

Maudie was just finishing breakfast when a rap sounded at the kitchen door. Hastily wiping a smear of marmalade from her mouth, she started to get up but she wasn't quick enough. The door flew open, revealing Harry Dempster on the step, accompanied by his two young children.

His daughter Rosie looked frightened and bedraggled. The buttons on her cardigan were done up wrongly and her wispy flaxen hair was already working loose from her stubby little plaits. Her little brother, on the other hand, looked excited and smug. He raced over to Maudie, whispering to her from behind his hand.

'Mummy done wees on the floor! Naughty Mummy!'

Maudie interpreted this to mean that his mother's membranes had ruptured. She patted the child on the head without comment.

'You'd best come, Nurse!' Harry Dempster said. 'I hope there's nothing wrong with our Phyl. She was a bit restless-like last night, wanting to scrub the kitchen floor, of all things, and now this!'

'We call that the nesting instinct,' Maudie told him. 'It's quite normal for women to feel the urge to prepare for the baby's arrival by going into a frenzy of activity. And if her waters have broken, that's a sign that the baby is on its way. I wish you'd called me as soon as labour began, though, Harry. I might have been off on my rounds this morning and you wouldn't have known where to find me.'

'That's just it, Nurse! She hasn't had any pains yet.'

'Then I'll pop over at once and see what's going on,' Maudie said. 'What about these two? They'll need to be kept out of the way until everything is done and dusted.'

'It's school for our Rosie, of course, and I've made an arrangement with Miss Rice to let our Bobby sit in for the day. He's due to start anyway as soon as he has his birthday and she says he can have this as a sort of trial run.'

'I'm going to play with plasticine!' Bobby told Maudie, his eyes shining.

'That's nice, dear. Now you'll have to run along, won't you, or you'll be late.'

'And then he'll get the cane,' Rosie said, speaking for the first time. Bobby's mouth went square and he let out a howl that would have stopped a mad bull in full charge.

'That's enough of that, you two!' Harry Dempster told them, taking each child by the hand. 'Do you want a clip round the ear? I wish you'd get over there, Nurse. Our Phyl's all alone over there in case you didn't know it!'

Maudie excused his rudeness, knowing that it stemmed from anxiety over his wife's safety. She was equally sure that his harsh response to his children's silliness was nothing more than an idle threat. 'Off you go, Harry. Do look in at lunch time to see how we're getting on.'

Maudie found Phyllis Dempster standing at her kitchen window, holding her bump and rocking back and forth. 'Harry tells me your waters have broken, but you've not had any pains yet. Is that right?'

'I'm having them now, Nurse,' Phyllis told her, between gritted teeth. 'Whoops! Here comes another one!'

'We'd better get you lying down, my girl! Is everything all ready for the baby?'

'Yes, and I've spread the rubber sheet on the bed, like always.'

'Right-ho! Up we go, then.'

Twenty minutes later Maudie was clipping the umbilical cord from a squalling baby girl, while Phyllis reached out for her, beaming.

'I can't believe my luck!' Phyllis said. 'I was in labour for fourteen hours with Rosie, and nine with our Bobby! Who would have thought it would all be over so fast!'

And with no damage to show for it, either, Maudie mused gratefully, as she waited for the afterbirth to be delivered. 'It won't be long now, Phyllis, and then I'll make you a nice hot cup of tea.'

'And lashings of toast to go with it please, Nurse! I'm that hungry I could eat a horse!'

'What are you going to call her?' Maudie asked, when they were drinking tea and casting admiring glances at the now-sleeping baby in the treasure cot beside the bed. Phyllis had washed the muslin drapes that hung from its wooden frame and trimmed it with yellow ribbon for, as she said, 'We couldn't know if it was a boy or a girl.' 'I'd have liked to call her after you, Nurse, seeing as you've done such a grand job of bringing me through it this time, but I don't know. It's a bit . . . '

'Old-fashioned, I know,' Maudie finished for her.

* * *

'Do you have a middle name, Nurse?'

'Yes, It's Grace, actually.'

'Ooh, I do like that! Grace! Grace Dempster. And I'll want you to be godmother, when the time comes,' Phyllis concluded.

Maudie was touched. 'Perhaps you'll want to discuss that with Harry first.'

'No need for that. As you know, there

has to be two godmothers and one godfather when it's a girl. We've already asked my Mum and Harry's brother, so that leaves one godmother to find.'

'Then I'll be proud to stand,' Maudie said. 'Now, if you feel safe staying alone, I'll trot along. I'll stop in to see Harry on my way past the garage, and I'll pop in later to check on you and Baby Grace. Is there anything else I can do for you before I leave?'

'I wouldn't mind another bit of toast!' Phyllis said, grinning. 'And there's a thermos in the kitchen cupboard if you'd like to leave me a brew.'

Maudie went on her way, rejoicing in a job well done. Harry Dempster was relieved and delighted when she called at the garage to tell him the good news.

'Thank the Lord for that!' he muttered, wiping a tear from his cheek and leaving an oily streak behind. 'I felt sure something was wrong when she . . . well, you know what happened.'

'No, no, Harry; everything is quite in order. No two labours are alike, you know, and your wife is delighted that she's got off so lightly this time. Now, what I want to know is, what plans have you made for Phyllis to have her nine days in bed? Knowing her as I do, she'll want to be up and doing in no time, especially with the young ones wanting her attention, but her body must have time to recover.'

'My sister's promised to come and stay for a few days, Nurse. That should set Phyllis right.'

'Does she have to come far?'

'No, just from Brookfield. If I can get hold of her now she'll probably come on the afternoon bus. They're not on the phone but I can ring the greengrocer's at the corner of her street and someone will get a message to her.'

'Her husband won't mind her being away for that long?'

Harry made a wry face. 'Poor old Sid copped it at El Alamein, Nurse. Our Edie does cleaning work for a living, but her ladies will just have to manage without her. Old Ma Logan may be a bit of a hard case, but she's always been kind enough to Edie, and she's not afraid to turn to and do a bit of dusting herself, her being a lodging house landlady.'

'Mrs Logan!' Maudie said thoughtfully.

'Do you know the old girl, then, Nurse?'

'We've met. Well, I must be on my way, and leave you to phone your sister. I'll pop in to the house later to check on Phyllis and your new daughter.'

* * *

'I'm Nurse Rouse,' Maudie said when she returned to the house later that afternoon, although the introduction was hardly necessary when she was wearing her uniform dress and cap. The woman who opened the door bore a distinct resemblance to Harry Dempster and must be Edie Dempster as was. The man had omitted to give Maudie his sister's surname.

'Oh, I know who you are,' the woman said, standing back to allow Maudie to pass into the house. 'You found poor Mr Swain, didn't you? He was a lovely man. I was so sorry to hear that he'd died, and in such a terrible way, too.'

Was Maudie to be forever branded as the unfortunate who discovered the corpse of Cyril Swain? Still, this at least gave her an introduction to the subject, because she had questions for this woman. First things first, though, she told herself, as she smiled and nodded to the baby's aunt.

'You go on up Nurse and make sure they're all right. Such a lovely little baby, and I can't believe that our Phyllis had such a short labour. You must have a magic touch.'

'Unfortunately I don't have any control over these things,' Maudie told her, 'but yes, I was pleased for Mrs Dempster's sake the way things worked out.'

'I expect you'll fancy a cup of tea. I've got the kettle on. I'll put one in your hand when you come back down and take one up to Phyllis, if she's awake.'

'That would be lovely,' Maudie said. She really didn't want any tea, but she did want to start the woman talking about Mrs Logan and Cyril Swain. When she had performed a few minor tasks and satisfied herself that all was well with her patient and her new baby she returned downstairs, ready for what her mother would have referred to as a good old chinwag.

17

'You work for Mrs Logan, I understand,' Maudie said, eager to get down to business.

'Yes, that's right,' Edie said. 'Her, among others. I have to make a living somehow, and it's not that easy for a woman to find work, now the men are back. I worked in a munitions factory during the war and enjoyed that, but there's nothing like that for me now.'

'Have you ever considered going in for nursing? There will always be work available in that field.'

Edie made a wry face. 'I haven't the qualifications to get in. I left school at fourteen and started out as a shop assistant in a little corner shop down the end of our street. Anyway, I don't think I could face it. My, you must have seen some sights, Nurse, especially during the war. Of course, I bet none of that was as bad as coming across poor Mr Swain the way you did.'

This gave Maudie the opportunity she'd been waiting for. 'Did you meet him when he was staying with Mrs Logan?'

'I did see him coming and going, yes.'

'But not to speak to?'

Edie hesitated. 'Actually, there was this one time. I had to do his room and I didn't know if he was in there or not, so I knocked on his door. There was no answer so I went in and found him sitting in a chair, all hunched over and weeping.'

'Weeping!'

'Yes. Sobbing like a baby, he was. I wanted to go and put my arm around him, to comfort him, like, but I didn't dare. So I just stood there like a lemon and said, 'Is there anything I can do, Mr Swain? Would you like me to fetch someone?' But he just shook his head and said it was too late. 'Too late for what?' I asked, but he just kept sniffing and muttering so I went away in the end.'

'And that's all he said? He didn't come out with anything else?'

'Nothing that made any sense. Something about Teddy, or Neddy, all dead now. Oh, yes, and he seemed to think I was somebody called Susan, because just as I was closing the door I heard him tell me he was sorry.'

'And what did you think he meant by that?' Maudie wondered.

Edie shrugged. 'I suppose he was apologizing for breaking down like that and crying in front of me. You know what men are like. They don't go in for a lot of emotional stuff.'

'Have you told this to the police?'

'Well, no. I mean, what is there to tell? The poor old chap was upset about something but what good would it do for me to broadcast that? Better let him rest in peace, I say.'

'I don't suppose he is resting peacefully,' Maudie said. 'I know I won't be able to settle until they catch whoever it was who killed him. And as far as I know they haven't found his people, whoever they are. He may have a wife somewhere, wondering what's happened to him and fretting because he hasn't come home.'

'That's hardly likely, is it, Nurse? That murder's been in all the papers. Surely somebody would have seen that.'

'I'm not so sure that his name's been in the papers, though. In the beginning nobody knew who he was.' Maudie had a newspaper clipping at home in which Cyril Swain was described as '*an unknown man, found dead at Llandyfan, a quiet country village on the border between England and Wales. Foul play suspected*.'

Suspected, my foot, she had thought on reading that. If they'd seen what I saw they'd jolly well have known he didn't strangle himself!

'You don't really think I should go to the police, do you, Nurse?' Edie looked anxious. 'I don't want them asking me a lot of silly questions.'

Maudie thought she understood. Like a lot of people who worked at a variety of jobs, Edie probably didn't declare all her earnings to the taxman. As a consequence, she probably spent half her time looking over her shoulder in case she was found out.

'Perhaps it doesn't matter,' she murmured. 'As you say, the poor man didn't really say anything sensible.' But her mind was whirling as she said it. She knew who Teddy was; at least, she recalled that he was the young man in one of Swain's snapshots.

She was still thinking about this when she went into Mrs Hatch's shop, looking for something tasty for her tea.

'Hello, Nurse! How's life treating you?'

She looked up from the shelf of tinned goods to find Dick Bryant standing at her elbow.

'Oh, hello, Constable. I'm quite well, thank you. I'm just trying to decide between Spam or corned beef and neither one holds any great appeal.'

'I hope you've got over your nasty experience,' he told her.

Maudie smiled. 'More or less, thank you. Have you made any progress in finding the man who killed him?'

'We're working on it, Nurse. We have learned a bit about Mr Swain, though. The poor old boy came from Devon. He was a veteran of the Great War. Imagine surviving the Somme, only to finish up dead in Llandyfan.'

'Mm.'

'I don't suppose you've heard any snippets of gossip on your rounds, have you? Any clue at all would be welcome.'

Maudie scratched one eyebrow. 'I forget where I heard it, but I did hear the name Susan mentioned. Not that it means much.'

'Oh, that's his wife,' Bryant said. 'We've managed to locate her. She's still living down in Devon.'

Maudie opened her eyes wide. 'Oh, that's good, then, isn't it? Has she been able to tell you what he was doing here? Has she any idea who might have killed him, and why?'

'Whoa, steady on, Nurse!' Bryant said, laughing. 'Unfortunately, she can't tell us anything. She's in a nursing home, recovering from a severe stroke. Not only has she lost the power of speech, but she seems addled in her wits as well. The doctors don't hold out much hope of a speedy return to normal, if ever.'

'That's that, then, I suppose.' Maudie had nursed a number of stroke patients in her time, and although many of them had eventually returned to health, there were always an unlucky few whose condition had improved very little.

'Perhaps it's a blessing in disguise,' Bryant suggested. 'At least the poor soul has no idea that her husband's been murdered. She's been spared that, at least.'

'Is she all alone in the world now, I wonder?' Maudie said, remembering the mysterious Teddy.

'According to the matron of the nursing home they did have a son, but he was killed in action during the war. He piloted Wellington bombers, she thought.'

'Did he leave a widow, do you suppose?'

'He wasn't married, as far as Matron knew. We did ask, Nurse. The police do know their job, you know.'

'Of course.' Maudie's face turned pink. She knew she had a bit of a cheek asking all these questions, but she did have a vested interest in the outcome. Still, in for a penny, in for a pound.

'What about poor Miss Plummer? Have you made any progress there?'

Bryant shook his head. 'Miss Rice

spoke to the children at assembly and asked for the boy who saw that man at the school to speak up. There were no takers. Then she appealed to any child who might have seen a strange man at the gate to let us know at once. Still nothing. After that all she could do was give them the usual lecture about not taking sweets from strangers and let them return to their classrooms. I should have thought they'd been only too willing to help trace the chap who tried to harm their Miss Plummer, but likely they're all scared half out of their wits.'

'I still think that Smith has something to do with all this,' Maudie said stubbornly. 'Can't you haul him in for questioning?'

'He's been thoroughly investigated, and we're satisfied that he's who he says he is. He's a rep for a firm based in Bradford, selling stationery. We've contacted them and they vouch for him unreservedly. Apparently he joined them right after he left the army, and he's worked for them ever since.'

Maudie had to be satisfied with that,

but when she went to bed that night various scenarios chased through her mind. Like it or not, men who joined the army were taught how to kill, which was necessary in time of war. Had Smith received commando training? It certainly seemed as if an experienced killer had murdered Cyril Swain. The big question, however, was what motive he could possibly have had . . .

18

Maudie arrived at the school, hoping for the best. If the mothers had been doing their stuff, the outbreak of head lice should be contained by now. Her mission today was to check the children's heads to see if this had been accomplished.

Pushing open the gate to let herself into the playground, she was surprised to see the caretaker, armed with a whistle, supervising a physical training class. Little girls were energetically skipping and bowling hoops, while a number of boys stood in an orderly row, twirling wooden clubs in circles.

'Hello,' Maudie greeted him. 'I didn't expect to see you here, Mr Cox. At least, not in charge of this mob.'

He regarded her rather sadly, she felt. 'You haven't heard, then. Miss Plummer has left us.'

'No! Is she all right?'

'Physically, yes, but she's gone to her

parents in Maidenhead. They were horrified when they heard what had happened and they insisted she stay with them to recuperate.'

'I see. And where does that leave you?'

'As you see, I've taken her place.' He broke off to shout at a grinning urchin. 'None of that, Ronnie Pope! You'll have his ear off if you're not careful. Just get back to what you're supposed to be doing!' He turned back to Maudie. 'Just until the end of term, that is. I'm told that the Board will review the situation then. It all depends whether Emma is coming back or not, of course. Mind you, there's some folk around here who think I'm the one who attacked her, just to frighten her off, leaving the job open for me.'

'Surely not!' But Maudie knew how village tongues could wag, and she felt sorry for the man. He had given up a decent career to go and serve king and country and he had returned to England, only to find himself jobless. He had taken on honest labour to support himself, and now it had come to this. Life was so unfair at times.

'I suppose you've come to do another inspection,' Cox said. 'Our time's just about up here, anyway. I'll get them back inside in two shakes and you can do your stuff.'

* * *

Practicing shallow breathing, Maudie bent over one little head after another, trying not to inhale the pungent odour of the noxious liquid that had been used to destroy the lice. Thankfully no horrid little beasties were found hiding in the assortment of curls, but there were still some nits holding on grimly to the hair on a number of pupils.

'Your heads are looking cleaner today,' she told the assembled children, 'but we're not out of the woods yet. You must ask your mummies to keep on with the toothcombs. Do you understand me?' Nods of agreement greeted this ultimatum.

'Right then, Mr Cox. I believe we're finished here. I'll go on to the big class now. If you happen to notice anything I should know about, don't hesitate to tell me.'

She was referring to a fresh outbreak of nits, of course, but to her surprise some of the youngsters seemed to think she meant something else. She noticed an exchange of frowns and head shaking, and young Lily Willis seemed to be doing a good job of gnawing her fingers down to the bone.

'We're not biting our fingernails, are we?' Maudie demanded, gently removing the child's fingers from her mouth. 'Bitten nails don't look very nice, dear. If you can't stop it we may have to paint them with some nasty-tasting stuff.'

'Don't care!' Lily spluttered.

'No back answers, Lily,' Mr Cox said gently, rewarded with a scowl that rivaled the expression worn by the gargoyle perched on the outer wall of the church. Maudie said nothing more, saddened that the formerly happy little girl now seemed nervous and angry. Obviously there was something wrong in the Willis home, and she wished she could get to the bottom of it, but how?

Cycling on to her next appointment she mulled this over, going on to think about the attack on Emma Plummer. It was just as well that the girl had gone to stay with her parents. Removing her from the scene of the crime to the home of her childhood where she felt secure was a good thing. And if she was too distressed by what had happened to her — and who would not be — then her parents were in the best position to find professional help for her. Maudie suspected that doctors who dealt with disturbances of the mind would still be run off their feet as they attempted to help patients who had suffered during the war, but surely a victim of a murder attempt would take precedence?

A murder attempt! Everyone assumed that Emma would have died but for the timely intervention of the Cubs and their leaders. But had the attacker really meant to kill the girl, or was it just a warning? And was this man and the killer of Cyril Swain one and the same? It could be a copycat crime. Someone totally different might have planned a sexual assault on the girl, expecting that Swain's killer would be blamed.

And why Emma? The rapist might have picked on the first woman or girl who passed by his hiding place, and in that case the poor young teacher had simply been in the wrong place at the wrong time. If for some reason the man had targeted Emma in particular, he could not have known that she would take the short cut through the woods.

'Rats!' Totally absorbed in her thoughts, Maudie found that she had cycled a good half mile past the lane where she should have turned in. 'Get a grip, Rouse!' she advised herself. Fantasizing about solving a murder mystery was all very well, but her job had to come first.

The patient she had called to see had given birth six weeks earlier, and both mother and child had come through the ordeal without complications. Now, however, the young mother was far from well, and Maudie believed that she was suffering from postnatal depression. She was confirmed in this diagnosis when the woman's husband, cradling his son in his arms, answered the door.

'We can't go on like this!' he burst out, when Maudie was barely inside the kitchen. Looking around the room, she was forced to agree. The sink was filled with unwashed dishes; every surface was piled high with laundry, newspapers and baby equipment; and a nasty smell drew attention to a pail in the corner where used nappies were piled high.

'I came home from work yesterday and found her lying in bed, with poor little Clark here howling the place down. She obviously hadn't done a stroke of work all day. And now look at us! I had to stay off work today but it's imperative I go into the office tomorrow for an important meeting or I'll get the sack! And then where will we be? You tell me that, Nurse!'

Maudie rolled up her sleeves. 'Clark looks as though he's about to fall asleep, Mr Allen. Why not put him down while I tidy up a bit, and then we'll have a chat about your Clarice, shall we?'

By the time the man had returned to the kitchen, Maudie had filled the sink with hot, soapy water and was making inroads into the pile of crockery. She handed him a tea towel. He looked at it in disbelief. 'What do you expect me to do with this?' he asked.

'I thought you might like to dry these crocks for me,' she told him, receiving an indignant glare in response.

'That is not my job, Nurse.'

'It's not mine, either,' Maudie snapped, 'but I'm doing it. So just get on with it, will you?'

They worked wordlessly together until the kitchen was put to rights. Then, over a cup of tea, she gave him a piece of her mind.

'Giving birth is a traumatic event in itself, Mr Allen. Combined with all the hormonal changes in a woman's body and the sleepless nights that follow Baby's arrival, that can lead to depression. And I understand that your wife worked as a secretary in a busy office before she was married. There she had the company of other women, as well as a pay packet that was hers to spend as she chose. Ever since you were married a year ago she's been at home all day, doing repetitive tasks and trying to cope with being pregnant as well. It's no wonder she's become depressed.'

'So this is all my fault, is it?' he demanded.

'That's not what I'm saying, Mr Allen. It's not a question of fault. It's simply that your wife has become overwhelmed by all these changes in her life and she needs help, and time to adjust. In a way it's unfortunate that little Clark came along so soon after the wedding.'

'But she wanted this baby!'

'I'm sure she did, Mr Allen, and I feel sure that everything will turn out well before long. In the meantime, I suggest you take your wife to see Dr Mallory, who may be able to prescribe something to help her over this hurdle.'

'I hardly think so, Nurse. That costs money, and I've already splashed out far too much on providing for this baby of hers!'

Maudie controlled her temper with difficulty. Getting to her feet, she announced that she had better look in on his wife before she left.

'And tell her to pull herself together and get moving!' Allen said. 'Just look at the time, will you? I've had no dinner!'

'When I come back down I'll teach you how to boil an egg,' Maudie told him, laughing at the man's stupefied expression.

* * *

'A curse on all men!' Maudie moaned as she pedalled down the lane. At times like this she was thankful she'd stayed single. In many cases the traditional division of labour between husband and wife worked well. The man worked outside the home to provide for the family; his wife kept a comfortable home for him to return to, with all his needs provided for. But surely marriage should also provide emotional support as well? The new demands being placed on Clarice Allen weren't to be solved by her husband telling her to buck up!

19

Len Frost stared at Maudie quizzically. 'Let me get this straight, Nurse. You want to inspect the accommodation we offer our guests here? Is this some kind of new health and safety requirement? I can assure you that my Dora does a thorough job of cleaning these premises, and I defy anyone to say otherwise.'

Maudie hesitated before deciding to take him into her confidence. 'I'd better explain,' she began.

'Yes, I think you had better,' the landlord said.

'This is just between you and me,' she said, tapping the side of her nose. 'It's about that John Smith you've had staying here. I do believe there's more to him than meets the eye.'

'Is that so? Well, Nurse, if you want to talk to him you're out of luck. He's gone again and I don't know when he'll be back. He's been here several times now, but never on a regular basis, like. He just puts in an appearance, we put him up, and then he's off until the next time. Anyway, if you're hoping to do a bit of detective work you're too late. The bobbies have already looked into him and he's come up clean.'

'I know that. Dick Bryant told me. I'd just like to have a look round his room, if I may. Please, Len, look at this from my point of view. I found poor Mr Swain's body. Then I had to help that poor little Emma after she was attacked in that very same place. Surely you can see why I have an interest in this? The police have had no success in solving these crimes and they've got me rattled. Probably the police have got it right, and this Smith is all he appears to be. I'd just like to rule him out in my own mind, that's all.'

Playing to the gallery, Maudie took out her handkerchief and dabbed at her eyes. Apparently the ruse worked, for Len's demeanour changed immediately.

'Oh, all right, Nurse. You might as well go up. I don't see what harm it can do. Anything to oblige a lady. Come on through.' He lifted the flap on the bar and Maudie hastened in before he could change his mind.

The Royal Oak was an ancient hostelry and there was a warren of rooms beyond the public bar and snug. Long ago it had been a coaching inn with accommodation for overnight travellers, as well as a livery stable in the walled yard.

'It's all right, Dora. Just showing Nurse upstairs,' Frost called as they went past what was evidently the kitchen quarters.

'Right-ho!' came an answering shout, accompanied by the clattering of pots and pans.

They climbed a flight of stairs, reaching a long passageway that branched off in two directions. 'The guest rooms are along here,' Len said, unlocking a door. Finding herself in a narrow hallway, Maudie noted another steep flight of stairs descending to what must be an outside door, the same entrance where she had previously observed John Smith going in. Naturally the people who stayed here would not be permitted to have access to the pub's private rooms. By the same token the Frosts would not necessarily be privy to the comings and goings of the guests themselves.

'This is where Smith stayed last time,' Len said, throwing open a door. 'My Dora's had a good clean since he left, so you won't find much to write home about. Never mind! You have a good look around, Nurse, and when you've finished you can just let yourself out down there. No need to come back through the bar.'

Maudie thanked him and looked around her. The place was clean and tidy, but it was hardly the Ritz. An old iron bedstead dominated the room. The maroon colour of the eiderdown and matching bedspread clashed horribly with a scarlet blanket folded at the foot of the bed. A tiny bedside rug, a wooden chair and a battered chest of drawers were the only other furnishings. Apparently patrons were supposed to hang their clothing on the single hook on the back of the door.

Maudie lifted a corner of the spread, stooping to peer under the bed. There was nothing there but a chamber pot, emblazoned by a stylized union jack. The drawers in the chest were bare. Remembering something she'd read in one of her beloved mystery novels, she pulled out each in turn, but nothing was taped to the underside of any. She struggled to replace them, sucking a finger where a splinter of wood had scratched her in the process.

There was nothing behind the gingham curtains. There was no fireplace in the room and no visible sign of any floorboards having been removed recently. And why should there be? What a waste of time this had been.

'You're a fool, Maudie Rouse!' she told herself. 'Looking for clues like a schoolgirl in an Angela Brazil book. Madcap Maudie, Heroine of the Fourth Form.' What on earth was she doing here? Len Frost must think she was an absolute idiot. She bustled down the stairs and let herself out into the sunlit yard.

Yet somehow she could not let go of the idea that there was something wrong about John Smith. Some primeval instinct told her that she must not become complacent about him if he ever returned to Llandyfan.

* * *

Mindful of the fact that her job was more important than wasting time playing sleuth, Maudie went to call on the vicar's wife. She found that lady busily pricing items that had been donated for the next jumble sale.

'Just look at some of these things,' Mrs Blunt mourned, holding a threadbare skirt up to the light. 'Most of them are only fit for the ragbag. I suppose someone could cut this up and use the good bits to make cushion covers or something, but people are so fed up with all that making do and mending of the war years, I don't know who'd want to bother.'

'Certainly not me,' Maudie replied, with a cheerful grin. 'How would you feel about starting a mothers and babies group in the parish?'

'What did you have in mind, Nurse? I'd like to help, but I don't know where I could find the time to take on anything new.'

'Oh, it wouldn't involve much. Just giving us the use of the parish hall one afternoon a week, or once a month even, when it's not in use for anything else. Perhaps the Mothers' Union could provide tea and biscuits, just as long as they understand that not everyone who might come is Church of England. I want this group to be open to any and all of my patients, regardless of church affiliation.'

'And you feel that there's a need for this sort of gathering?'

'Yes, I do. Being stuck at home with a new baby and other preschoolers can be so isolating. I've a new mum right now — naming no names — who is in dire need of moral support. If she could get a break from the daily routine once in a while, perhaps to exchange notes with others in her situation, it might do her the world of good. And in the long run everyone would benefit: husbands, children; marriages, even.'

Mrs Blunt smiled. 'I'll have a word with Harold, Nurse, but I'm sure he'll be all for it. Now, then, what do you suppose we can do with all these odd socks? I can't think what made people donate them.'

Maudie wheeled her bicycle home,

feeling pleased with herself. With this new project she could kill several birds with one stone, but the overriding need was to help Clarice Allen. She would have to be clever about it. A problem with these village gatherings was that almost everyone was related to others in the group, or had at least gone to school with practically everybody. A newcomer like Clarice was left out in the cold. It wasn't that the other women were standoffish, just that it was natural for them to gravitate towards those with whom they had prior relationships.

Maudie suddenly thought of Daisy Larke. She and Clarice should get along like a house on fire. Both were first-time mothers, and little Richard was only a few months older than baby Clark. As time went by the tiny boys could become friends.

Clark. What a name to go to bed with, Maudie groaned. Probably named after the cinema heartthrob, Clark Gable, of course. That gave her another idea. She must invite Greta Black to join the group. The teenager might be shy in front of all those women, yet she was soon to become a mother herself, when she would need all the help she could get. And if it turned out that Clarice Allen was a keen filmgoer, or had been, before she found herself confined to home with her new son, the pair would have something in common. Greta might be persuaded to babysit for the Allens, allowing the couple to have the occasional outing without having the baby in tow.

Delighted with her plan, Maudie gave herself a mental pat on the back.

20

Maudie stood still on a deserted stretch of road and screamed until she was red in the face. Then, feeling somewhat better, she mounted her bicycle and continued on her way.

The day had begun well enough. She had awakened just before her alarm clock went off, feeling refreshed. While she was dressing she thought she heard the letterbox rattle and wondered why the post had come so much earlier than usual. When she went to investigate she found a note on the doormat, obviously delivered by hand because the message was written in pencil on a sheet torn from a school copybook. Some labouring chap must have left it on his way to work.

She looked at the grubby piece of paper, biting her lip. 'Come at once. Miscarriage', it read, followed by an address beyond the furthest reaches of her district. She knew she didn't have an expectant mother there, but that meant nothing. Very often an early miscarriage occurred before a woman realized that she was pregnant, which could be the case here. Maudie had her day already planned but this had to take precedence, for if a woman was in trouble and all alone in some remote place she needed help.

She wished she had been up in time to catch whoever had brought the note. Then she might have been able to find out more. Very few people had a telephone in the home, usually relying on a public telephone kiosk when they needed to contact the outside world. Thus there was no point in calling directory enquiries in an attempt to contact the woman, whoever she was. Maudie realized with a start that she hadn't been given a name, just an address, Woodside Farm.

After a long, weary ride into the teeth of a brisk wind she dismounted in a rutted farmyard, holding her bicycle between herself and a cross-looking dog. The sound of his barking brought a burly man to the door of an enormous barn. Maudie approached with caution. The man looked far too old to be the husband of a pregnant woman. Possibly her patient was the wife of a farm labourer, living in a nearby cottage?

The man looked at her in puzzlement when he heard why she had come. 'Pregnant, Nurse? Ain't nobody pregnant here, not 'less you count that old sow of mine, ready to farrow. You've come to the wrong place, gal!'

'Isn't this Woodside Farm, then?'

'That it was, last time I looked.'

Maudie showed him the scrap of paper, which caused him to scratch his head.

'It says Woodside Farm right enough, but like I said, there's nobody expecting here. Come to the kitchen door while I ask my missus if she knows of anyone hereabouts needing a nurse. Mebbe in the heat of the moment they gave this address as a landmark to look out for on your way to wherever it is you're supposed to go.'

But the grey-haired woman enveloped in a floral overall, shook her head decisively. 'It's like my Jim told you,

Nurse. There's nobody within miles in the family way.'

'It could be one of them gypsies,' Jim said, 'except I haven't seen any in these parts of late.'

'They look after their own,' his wife said. 'They don't hold with what they call Giorgio ways. You know that, Jim. Well, Nurse, I don't know what else to say. Seems to me you've come on a wild goose chase.'

Maudie was forced to agree. After refusing the offer of a cup of tea, she started back the way she had come, gingerly keeping an eye on the dog that had followed her back down to the lane. She had gone a full mile before she stopped to give vent to her frustration. There was nothing for it but to return to Llandyfan, with her day in disarray.

Her temper was not improved when she approached the railway bridge, where several small boys were leaning over the guardrail, elbowing each other and staring down at an approaching train. Playing truant, she thought grimly. Well, that was no business of hers, although she suspected they were up to no good.

'Come on out of that!' she called. 'I hope you lot aren't playing chicken!' By their shamefaced expressions she knew she had guessed correctly. This was a stupid game, beloved of young boys, in which the players remained at the railing while the train puffed its way under the bridge, belching steam and noxious fumes in its wake. Choking and gasping, the participants would be forced to flee. The one who stayed in place the longest was declared the winner.

Delivering a lecture on the folly of getting their lungs full of poisonous substances, Maudie failed to notice that a large elm tree was swaying dangerously in the wind. A fresh gust brought it crashing down across the track below, accompanied by gasps of horror from the boys.

'Miss! Miss! The train's going to crash into that tree! We have to tell somebody!'

But there was no time for that. As they watched, the engine crashed into the tree with a great cracking sound, driving the trunk ahead of it. When the train finally shuddered to a stop, one of the three passenger coaches detached itself from the rest and seemed to flop on its side in slow motion under Maudie's horrified gaze. Looking down at her hands, she saw that she had driven her nails into the palms, leaving a series of small gouges. She braced herself for action.

'Run and fetch help, boys. Let someone know that the train has been derailed!' They raced off willingly enough, but heaven alone knew how long it might take for help to come. She was a nurse, wasn't she? It was up to her now. Plucking her bag from the basket on her bicycle, she hurried down the embankment towards the train, slipping and sliding as she went. Later she was to wonder why she'd taken her bag with her, save for the fact that it could not be left unattended. There was very little in it that could be useful in dealing with the sort of injuries she was likely to encounter at the scene down below.

Shouts and moans reached her eyes when she arrived at the train. 'I'm a nurse,' she informed the guard, who came hurrying forward to greet him. 'I've sent some boys for help, but meanwhile I'd better see what I can do for anyone who's been hurt. Is anyone bleeding badly? I suppose we don't happen to have a doctor on board?'

'There's a chap who's with the St John's Ambulance, Nurse. He's putting splints on a man who seems to have a broken leg. And there's a lot of cuts and bruises that'll want seeing to, but in the main I'd say we've been lucky. We hadn't got up to speed yet, on account of we stopped back at the halt, and I reckon that's what saved us. If we'd been going much faster it could have been a different story.'

Maudie stopped to comfort the engineer, who was sitting beside the embankment in a state of shock. 'I've never had an accident in all my years on the railway,' he mumbled. 'This would have to happen now, just when I'm coming in for retirement. If I lose my pension I don't know how I'll manage.'

'It wasn't your fault,' she told him. 'That tree came down right out of the blue and there wasn't a thing you could do about it. I shall stand up at the inquiry and say so. The powers that be are bound to call for any witnesses.' The man continued to rock back and forth in distress, repeating his mantra over and over. 'Not in all my years. Never a problem till now.'

Maudie was distracted by a scream coming from the stricken carriage. It was not a corridor train and she had to inch her way along the track until she came to the right compartment. Clambering in past the broken door, she found a distraught woman hunched over on the floor with her hands clamped over a battered felt hat.

'We've been bombed again!' she shrieked. 'It's that rotten Luftwaffe. Mr Churchill tried to tell us they were done for, but I didn't believe him, and I was right!' She reared up, shaking her fist at the sky. 'You got my home last time, you rotten devils; smashed everything I owned. Wasn't that enough for you? No, you had to come back to finish the job. Just when I was going to Bournemouth to have a nice little holiday with my sister.'

What the woman needed was a dose of tranquillizer to take her into merciful oblivion until her system had recovered from the trauma, but Maudie had nothing to give her. Delegating another passenger to sit with the woman to prevent her throwing herself about, she moved on to the next patent.

In her training days she had worked in the casualty department and had had to deal with all the attendant consequences of Saturday nights in a big city, so she was able to take this crash in her stride. Between them, she and the first aid man had everything under control by the time the ambulances arrived.

'Can we give you a lift somewhere?' one of the attendants enquired. Maudie sighed. 'I really wish you could, but I have to go back the way I came. I've left my bicycle up there and I don't want it nicked. Besides, I'll need it for work tomorrow.'

Bent almost double, she scrambled back up the embankment, losing her footing once or twice. Tutting, she noticed a large blood stain on her uniform dress; that would take some getting out, she knew.

Almost two hours and several miles later, she found herself entering Llandyfan village, more than ready for a soak in a hot bath. 'What a day!' she groaned, as her cottage came in sight. 'At least it's over now, and nothing else is likely to happen this late in the day!' She was wrong.

21

Maudie cycled past the parish hall without stopping. She felt ready to collapse and there was really no need to drop into her office. There were no notes to write up because she hadn't seen a single maternity patient. All she wanted to do now was to stretch out her tired limbs and let the distressing scenes of the train crash fade from her mind. A long soak in hot, scented bathwater might prevent sore muscles the following day.

While the tub was filling, she added a generous helping of bath salts from a green pottery rabbit that she had received at Christmas from a grateful patient. They were strongly scented and not really to her taste, but why look a gift horse in the mouth, she thought, as she shook in another few lumps. Or gift rabbit, as the case might be.

A furious pounding sounded at her cottage door. Sighing, she turned off the taps and struggled downstairs, thrusting her arms into her dressing gown as she went. She was surprised when the vicar's wife pushed her way into the tiny hall without waiting for an invitation.

'I'm sorry to burst in on you like this, Nurse, but I think you'd better come immediately.'

'What's up? Is someone hurt?' Please don't let it be someone in advanced labour!

'No, no, not that. I was just opening up the parish hall, ready for the Brownie meeting, which as you know happens after school today.' Mrs Blunt paused for breath.

Maudie's heart sank. She recalled that Miss Plummer acted as Tawny Owl for the pack: in other words assistant to the Brown Owl, Mrs. Marks. Now that the girl had gone away, this must have left a vacancy in the ranks. Surely to goodness Mrs Blunt didn't have Maudie earmarked as the replacement? She was happy enough to act as tester for the first aid badge that was so popular with the Scouts and Guides, but she couldn't see herself tiptoeing around a plaster-of-Paris mushroom, hooting, or whatever it was the Brownie leaders did.

'To cut a long story short,' Mrs Blunt said, 'I found the door to your office standing wide open. You didn't forget to lock up, did you, Nurse?'

Maudie had to think. She was always meticulous in locking the door to her little domain. Surely she hadn't slipped up now? 'I haven't been to the office today at all. I was called out first thing this morning and I dashed off straight away. I always bring my bag home at night, just in case.'

'Then I'm afraid someone must have broken in, Nurse. And what's worse, they've made quite a mess. I came to you first of all, but I really think this is a case for Dick Bryant. Will you come with me now?'

'I'll have to slip upstairs and put some clothes on. I was just running myself a bath and I'm in my petticoat. You go back in case the Brownies turn up, and I'll join you in a moment.'

When Maudie reached the parish hall,

she found Mrs Blunt standing guard at the office door. Inside, the place was indeed a mess. The drawers of her filing cabinet gaped open and the patients' record cards were scattered all over the desk and floor. Maudie moaned. 'Who would do a thing like this, Mrs Blunt? It'll take me forever to sort this lot out!'

'Has anything vital been taken?'

'I can't tell. I don't keep valuables here, and there are no pills or potions that anyone might want to steal. Nothing on the shelves seems to have been disturbed.' The two women stared at the neat stacks of towels, rubber sheets, jars of Epsom salts and all the other paraphernalia of Maisie's profession.

'Anyone home?' At the sound of Dick Bryant's voice the two women turned to face the door. 'I came as soon as I could, ladies. You've had a bit of trouble here, I see. Was anything taken?'

'We were just discussing that,' Maudie told him. 'Whoever it was seems to have concentrated on messing up my files!'

'And why should that be, do you think?'

Maudie spread her hands wide. 'Don't ask me! Patients' records are confidential, of course, but they don't hide any dark secrets. Just details of deliveries, birth weights, follow-up visits and so on. I do keep a book where I jot down dates and things having to do with any non-maternity dealings, like the recent nit inspection at the school.'

'Perhaps I could see that, Nurse?'

'Of course, although I doubt it will tell you much. Hang on a minute; it must be here somewhere.' But a brief search confirmed that the book was missing.

The sound of high-pitched chatter heralded the arrival of the first Brownies, who stared in fascination at the scattered documents.

'Look at the mess!' one said cheerfully. 'We can clear that up for you, Nurse, quick as a wink. We're supposed to do a good turn for somebody every day, you know.'

'Thank you all the same,' Maudie told the child, 'but this is something I'll have to do for myself.' She turned to Bryant. 'Aren't you going to dust for fingerprints or something?'

He shook his head. 'It's hardly worth bothering, seeing that nothing of value has been stolen. If you happen to come across your book you can let me know, but I expect you'll find it at home. As you say, why would anyone want notes about school head inspections?'

Maudie made it a rule never to take work home with her, or to keep records anywhere other than in her locked cabinet. Still, she was too tired to argue with the man. 'If you've seen all you want to see I'm going to shut the door on this lot and have a go at it tomorrow. All right?'

When she eventually returned to her cottage she found that the bath water was cold. Cursing, she pulled out the plug and let the water drain away. She had lost the urge to soak in soothing water. What she needed now was a meal, and one that didn't take much energy to prepare. Beans on toast should do the trick, but suddenly the thought of lighting the gas and waiting for toast to brown under the grill was just too much. Opening the can of Heinz baked beans, she attacked the contents with a spoon. That was one thing about beans; they tasted just as good eaten cold.

* * *

The next morning Maudie awoke, stiff and cold. Her eiderdown had slipped off during the night and was lying on the floor, leaving her covered with nothing more than a sheet and a threadbare blanket. One of these days she meant to replace all her bedding with lovely new items, but there was no point in thinking about it yet. Bedding cost coupons and there was nothing in the shops anyway.

She got up slowly, reluctant to face the day. She had two choices. Either she could do her neglected home visits, or she could tidy up her office. It didn't take her long to come to a decision. There was nothing pressing when it came to fieldwork. No imminent confinements, no brand-new mothers and babies to check on. She could continue her rounds in the afternoon with no harm done. The office should be made a priority, not only because the records must be put in order without delay, but also because the mystery of who had invaded the place, and why, was irritating her. As she tackled her boiled egg she suddenly realized that she should have mentioned her hoax call to Dick Bryant. The stress of the long ride and the train wreck, followed by the discovery of the break-in, had quite driven it from her mind. Now she put two and two together, frowning.

Someone had sent her off on a wild goose chase to get her out of the way while he — or she — broke into her office. It seemed a bit extreme. Why not keep watch until they saw her setting off on her regular rounds?

In her office she stared glumly at the lock on the filing cabinet, which had been jimmied open. Could these locks be mended, or would the whole cabinet have to be replaced? Meanwhile, she could at least put the cards in alphabetical order, which was a tiresome job.

As she worked she looked for any that had gone missing. Unfortunately there was no master list of the patients she had dealt with, past and present. If any of the cards had been taken, she might not realize it until she wanted to refer to a specific case and was unable to find the information she wanted.

A cough at the door made her sit up sharply. A tall, skinny man stood there, looking as startled as she was herself. 'Looks like the wind blew in here,' he observed, waving a work-roughened hand at the mess on the floor.

'Goodness, you startled me!' Maudie said. 'Creeping about like that! Who are you? What do you want?'

'Sorry, it must be my plimsolls,' the man said, pointing to the worn canvas shoes on his feet. 'I'm Sid, the potman at the Royal Oak.'

'Oh, yes?'

'The gaffer sent me. He says, could you come and have a look at some chap upstairs. He reckons he's having fits, the chap that is, on account of he's shaking like a leaf and muttering to himself.'

'All right, tell Mr Frost I'll be there shortly. No peace for the wicked,' Maudie muttered.

22

'Oh, there you are, Nurse!' Len Frost's expression was grim. 'I'm glad you were able to come. I don't know what's the matter with that chap up there but I hope it's nothing catching.'

'What exactly is he complaining of, Mr Frost? Has he said anything to you?'

'Nothing that makes any sense, Nurse. Yesterday he was moaning on about being cold. Wanted to know if he could change to a room with a fireplace in it, if you please. Said he had a headache as well, but I thought that came about from having one too many in here, if you get my meaning.'

'But your potman says he's been having fits today.'

'Oh, you know Sid! None too bright at the best of times and he heard me say I hope Smith isn't one of them epileptics like a poor lady that stayed here once. She had a fit and bit her tongue something awful. No. This chap's not like that but he's shivering and shaking and he was sick all over my good Axminster rug, dirty devil. Didn't even offer to clean up after himself.'

'It sounds as if it could be flu,' Maudie said. 'I hope this isn't the start of an epidemic. That's all we need!'

'The chap muttered something about malaria, Nurse. He must have been rambling. We don't get that in England, do we? One of them nasty foreign diseases I thought.'

Maudie thought quickly. Could it be malaria? They hadn't learned much about tropical diseases in her training days, although she had a vague idea that malaria could be transmitted from a mother to her baby, either before or during delivery. Obviously that was not the case here.

'Have you rung Dr Mallory?' she asked.

Frost shook his head. 'I thought I'd let you have a look at the chap first. I didn't want to bring the old man all the way from Midvale unnecessarily. Smith wouldn't thank me for landing him with a doctor's bill, and he can get a nasty look in his eye at times, can Smith. Very nasty.'

'Leave it to me, then,' Maudie said. 'If I think it might be malaria I'll phone the doctor myself.'

'And then we'll be in quarantine, I suppose! That's all we need. Trade is bad enough without us being put out of business like we have the plague.'

'We'll just wait and see, shall we?' Households were put into quarantine to prevent the spread of infection when children came down with certain diseases such as measles or chickenpox that had to be reported to the authorities. Maudie didn't know if these rules applied to malaria that, as Frost had indicated, was seldom found in England. She hoped that old Doctor Mallory would be better informed.

She found Smith bathed in sweat, tossing and turning on his narrow bed. 'I'm Nurse Rouse,' she told him. 'The landlord has asked me to take a look at you. He tells me you may have malaria, is that right?'

A grunt was the only answer she received, but she could see that his breathing was laboured. 'We'll just put this under your tongue, shall we?' she said, taking a thermometer from her bag. As she suspected, he had a high fever. She gently pulled down his lower eyelid, noting that the white was yellowish in colour.

'Well?' Frost demanded, when she rejoined him in the bar. 'Is it malaria, Nurse?'

'That's for the doctor to say, Mr Frost. I'm a midwife, not a specialist in outlandish diseases. May I use your phone to call Dr Mallory?'

'If you must, Nurse. Leave the money in the box, if you don't mind.'

Maudie shot him an old-fashioned look. Local calls cost money but she wasn't about to pay for this out of her own pocket. She went into the kiosk and lifted the receiver.

'From what you say it could be malaria,' the doctor told her, when she had reported details of the patient's temperature, pulse, respiration and general condition. 'It's caused by a parasite that enters the body from the bite of an infected mosquito. I've treated a few men who contracted the disease while serving abroad during the war.'

'But the war has been over for two years, Doctor.'

'Ah, yes, but some of these parasites remain dormant in the liver for years and if they wake up, so to speak, the patient can have a relapse. I suppose I'll have to come and take a look at the fellow. At the Royal Oak in Llandyfan, you say?'

'That's right.'

'If I confirm your findings I'll prescribe quinine and you'll have to see that he takes it, Nurse.'

Oh, no you don't! Maudie thought, not quite daring to voice her displeasure. 'I'm a midwife, Doctor,' she said meekly.

'There's no need to remind me, nurse! I'm not quite senile yet. Tell me, now, how many nurses are there in your district?'

'Just me, Doctor.'

'And I suppose that if this damn fool Health Service takes effect next year you may be swamped with other staff in due course. But in the meantime, midwife or not, you seem to be the only trained person available, am I right?'

'I suppose so.'

'And how many deliveries have you pending?'

'Nothing immediate,' Maudie admitted.

'Then it wont hurt you to pop in for a few minutes each day, will it? If I remember rightly the inn is just a few minutes' walk from your office in the parish hall.'

'Yes, Doctor,' Maudie said.

'Len Frost looked up from his task of polishing tumblers when she emerged from the telephone kiosk. 'Did you catch the doc, Nurse?'

'Yes. He'll look in later today.'

'And will you be staying with the chap in the meantime?'

'I'm sorry, no. I have to go about my business. This has made me late as it is.'

'Then who's to look after him in the meantime? I don't want my Dora going in there and catching something nasty.'

'If it's malaria then Dora will be quite

safe. You can only get malaria from a mosquito bite. Dr Mallory has just confirmed that.'

'Ah, but what if it's not malaria, Nurse? Have you thought of that? As you said yourself you're not a doctor, so it could be anything. Cholera, say, or one of them nasty sailors' diseases.'

'Or leprosy, or bubonic plague!' Maudie snapped. 'I'm off now, Len. When the doctor gets here he'll be able to set your mind at rest. Meanwhile, there's nothing more to be done for the chap. Goodbye!'

Maudie let herself out into the street, fuming. However, she hadn't got very far down the lane when a thought occurred to her. She was in a perfect position to find out more about the mysterious Mr Smith. She could go back later and give him a bit of a wash, or remake his tumbled bed, and while there she could snoop around for clues. With any luck he might be delirious and start talking, and she might learn something useful there.

By the time she had calmed down she had managed to convince herself that it was only right and proper that, midwife or not, she should do what she could for the man. Once a nurse, always a nurse!

* * *

On her way into the parish hall, Maudie was accosted by Mrs Blunt. 'Is everything all right, Nurse? Only, I saw you dashing off without your bicycle and I wondered if there was an accident somewhere.'

'It's that Mr Smith,' Maudie replied. 'That rep who stays at the Royal Oak. He's not very well. Dr Mallory has promised to come and take a look at him. We think he's having a relapse of malaria.'

Normally Maudie would not have given details of a patient's condition to anyone, that being contrary to nursing ethics. However, Len Frost was in the know, which meant it would be all over the parish by now.

'Oh, yes, I've a cousin who gets that,' Mrs Blunt said.' It's a nasty thing while it lasts, and I'm told that if it's left untreated it can lead to kidney failure, coma or even death.'

'Did your cousin catch it during the war?'

'He's a missionary in India. Actually he's served in a few of those hot countries, where Europeans run the risk of dying with some nasty disease. Do you know, Nurse, my Harold once entertained thoughts of going to the mission field. He actually thought of spending the rest of his life in China. He was quite determined, and at the time I really believed that nothing would shake him.'

'It's a good thing he changed his mind, then,' Maudie said, grinning, 'or the two of you would never have met.'

'Oh, we were already married by then,' her friend said, 'but for once I put my foot down. You see, I did not experience a call to serve in Asia.'

'Men!' Maudie thought. It boggled the mind to think that any man would make such a life-altering decision in the cheerful expectation that his wife would meekly follow him into unknown dangers.

23

'Mallory here. I've been to see your man and I'm pretty sure it's malaria.'

'I see.' The telephone line was crackling and Maudie frowned at the receiver before continuing. 'Is he fit to be left alone, Doctor? Can't you put him in the cottage hospital?'

'I thought of that, Nurse, but they don't have a bed to spare. They're filled to overflowing because of that train derailment of yours. You and the man's landlady will just have to manage between you.'

'She isn't a nurse,' Maudie protested, knowing what Len Frost would make of that.

'My dear woman, any female worth her salt should be able to make a bed and sponge a patient down. I've left the quinine there. You should be able to deal with that.'

'Hello?' They had been cut off,

although whether the doctor had hung up, or there was a fault on the line, was anybody's guess.

'Dratted man!' she howled. Mallory had cast aspersions on the whole nursing profession, and on Maudie in particular, yet so many doctors seemed to think of themselves as little gods, with nurses as their handmaidens. She had memories of her training hospital where probationers were not allowed to address any doctor. Even if his clothes had been on fire they would have had to speak to a Sister, who in turn would relay the information to the doctor concerned.

'Which man is that?' Maudie hadn't heard Mrs Blunt padding up behind her in her soft shoes.

'Come to think of it, all men!'

'You sound fed up, Nurse. Would you like to come over to the rectory for a cup of tea? I can offer you freshly baked melting moments to go with it and you can unburden your worries onto me.'

'Now that's an offer I can't refuse,' Maudie said. 'The melting moments, I mean. And I suppose I've not much to complain about, really. It's only that some doctors are like Rumpelstiltskin; they demand one thing after another with never a word of thanks, and expect to be obeyed without question.'

'I suppose you could take that as a compliment, Nurse, don't you think? If the old boy thought you were incapable he wouldn't rely on you so completely.'

'Tcha!' growled Maudie.

Mrs Blunt smiled. 'I assume this has something to do with your malaria man? If it's all too much for you I could pop over and tidy him up a bit.'

'You're an angel in disguise, Mrs B, but I'm sure I'll be able to manage, thank you. Now, did you say something about little cakes that melt in the mouth?'

* * *

On her return to the Royal Oak, Maudie met Mrs Frost, who was carrying a pile of sheets. 'I looked in on him a while ago and he's soaked to the skin, Nurse. With sweat, that is; nothing worse, I mean. And what you're going to do about clean pyjamas I don't know. My Len only possesses the one pair, and those are in use right now. I'll be glad when this rationing business ends so I can replace his old ones. I'm that tired of mending and patching, like everybody else in England, I shouldn't wonder.'

'If Mr Smith doesn't have spares he'll have to sleep in his undies,' Maudie said. 'It won't do him any harm if he's sweating as much as you say.'

At that moment a woman entered the inn, saying something about having homegrown carrots for sale. 'I mustn't keep you,' Maudie said, removing a pair of sheets from Dora Frost's arms. 'I'll go on up and attend to our friend. I'll call you if I need you.'

'Right-ho, Nurse.'

Maudie took a quick look around the room. Smith was tossing about in the bed and mumbling. Was this her chance to look for clues? A battered suitcase stood in the corner, with what she took to be his samples case perched on top. Fortunately neither one was locked.

Having snapped open the clasps on the

briefcase, she quickly rifled through the contents. It appeared that John Smith was indeed a traveller in stationery goods, and the case held his samples. She saw pads of writing paper in three different sizes, with envelopes to match; plain postcards; notebooks with green mottled covers. A slightly larger book appeared to be his order book because it held the addresses of what she took to be offices or retail shops.

The only other item of interest was a half-finished handwritten letter beginning 'Dear Ruth.' That might yield some clues. Looking over her shoulder, Maudie folded it gently and stuffed it into her apron pocket. Feeling guilty, she reminded herself that nice people didn't read other people's letters. And nice people don't go around murdering elderly men, she told the voice in her conscience.

She had just opened the suitcase when the man in the bed shouted, 'Hey!', making her jump. 'You leave that case alone, missus! That's private.'

Maudie rallied quickly. 'I was just having a look to see if you have another pair of pajamas, Mr Smith. You have a high temperature and it's making you perspire. Those you have on are wringing wet. Can't you feel them?'

'So what if I can? Ain't no business of yours, woman.'

Maudie had dealt with recalcitrant patients before. 'That will do, Mr Smith! I'm your nurse, and I'm here to see that you do everything that's needed to enable you to return to health. Doctor Mallory has given me instructions, and I'm here to carry them out.'

Smith growled something under his breath, which she ignored, going back to the suitcase. It did indeed hold another suit of pajamas, a very fine pair in paisley silk. Perhaps those were not suitable under the circumstances. She folded them and put them back.

'Right, Mr Smith; let's get you out of those damp clothes. They really need a good wash but for now I'll hang them out on the line. In the meantime you'll have to put on your pants and vest.' Smith had other ideas, so rather than struggle to pull the vest over his head she pulled on his underpants and left it at that. At last, having made him as comfortable as she could, she left the room, promising to return later.

* * *

'Dear Ruth', the letter began. Now who was Ruth? A wife? His sister? Maudie frowned and read on. 'Here's hoping you are in the pink, as I am too.' Well, that was wrong, for a start! Malaria was no joke.

'My passage is booked and I'll see you in a few weeks if all goes according to plan. I have seen our little prize, only I can't get near it at present. There are too many nosy parkers around. I thought I had it once but it was the other one. Never mind, I'll . . . '

Frustrated, Maudie turned the letter over but the other side of the page was blank. Smith must have been interrupted before he could complete his letter, or perhaps he had set it aside when he began to feel unwell.

None of this made sense to Maudie. It seemed to be written in the sort of code used by two people who shared some information that they had to keep from others. It did sound as if the man was about to flee the country, but where was he going? And why? And was that any business of hers?

She wondered if she should take the letter to Dick Bryant, to be used in evidence against Smith if need be. But there was nothing in it that pointed to any wrongdoing and she would possibly be dismissed as a silly, imaginative woman. Maudie prided herself on being a practical person, full of common sense, which were ideal qualities in a nurse and midwife. She did not want that image to be distorted.

She thrust the letter back into her pocket and immediately pulled it out again, smoothing out the creases. She had to return the letter to Smith's briefcase and it wouldn't do for it to look crumpled, or he would suspect something. She wondered now if he had noticed her removing it.

Perhaps it was best to destroy the letter, in the hope that Smith would think he'd mislaid it somehow. If he had seen something and he later accused her, she could insist that he had been delirious, having nightmares if you like, and had only seen her searching for his clean clothing. On the other hand it might be best to keep the paper in a safe place, to be brought out later if it transpired that the police had an interest in him.

Could he have been the man who had done for poor Cyril Swain, and later attacked Miss Plummer in the woods? His hands had grasped Maudie's when she'd been tussling with him in an attempt to remove his perspiration-soaked garments and even in his illness his grip had been mighty. She shuddered now to think that those strong fingers might have choked the life out of an innocent man.

Was it wise for her to be alone in the room with him when she next went to see him? The people downstairs would never hear anything that was happening: the guest rooms were too far away. Perhaps she should ask Mrs Frost to accompany her the next time, or Mr Frost to wait on the landing, within call.

24

Summer was over at last, bringing with it cool nights and misty mornings. Rain dripped from the eaves into overflowing water barrels, and birds chirped dismally in cottage gardens. The gardens were full of goldenrod, purple Michaelmas daisies, and late roses, a sure sign that the war was over and done with. During those dark years every available patch of earth had been used for growing food; flowers had been a luxury then. The only vestiges of nature's glory had been the wildflowers in the ditches and hedgerows.

Maudie had been to deliver a baby in one of the cottages that stood in a row about a mile from the centre of the village. 'Another boy!' the exhausted mother had mourned, when the child made its appearance after several gruelling hours of labour. 'Ah, well; I suppose John will be pleased, but I did hope for a little girl this time. That makes six boys now, you know, Nurse.'

'You'll soon have your own football team if you go on like this,' Maudie quipped.

Her patient scowled. 'What, eleven children? Not on your life! Never again, I tell you, Nurse. I'm done with all this!' Despite her cross words she looked at the newborn dotingly.

Maudie busied herself with tidying away the signs of childbirth. She sympathized with the woman, of course she did, but preventing further additions to the family was problematic. Short of strict abstinence, there was no sure way of preventing conception and she told herself that she would probably be back in this very room the following year. Mrs Benson was one of those very fertile women who conceived easily.

Not for the first time, Maudie wondered why nature could not have arranged things better. There were women who longed desperately for a child but were still trying after years of marriage. Her thoughts went to Helen Willis. Why was she unable to conceive? Her failure to do so seemed to be causing trouble in that marriage, probably because the husband seemed to think it was a reflection on him, or his manhood.

As his wife had predicted, Seb Benson was delighted with his new son. When Maudie handed him the baby he kissed the little damp brow, glowing with pride and happiness.

'I don't know if your wife is all that pleased,' Maudie said, grinning to show that she wasn't serious. 'She tells me she was hoping for a little girl.'

'Oh, that's just talk, Nurse! Muriel doesn't mind what it is, so long as it has all its fingers and toes, which I assume this one has! Beside, there's always next time, eh?'

'Better not mention that right now!' Maudie grunted. 'Not unless you want that bedpan thrown at your head!'

Seb laughed. 'I'll just make Muriel a cup of tea, and then I'll go next door to Mum's to let her have the news. She'll be round here like a shot to have a look at the new one. She wanted to be with Muriel but there was nobody else to look after the boys. Jenny down the row said she'd have them, but she was out when I went to fetch her, and her man didn't know when she'd be back. Do you want me to walk you home, Nurse? It gets dark earlier these nights.'

'No, no. I'll be fine. It's not that far.' Maudie felt the need of some fresh air after being shut in the Bensons' tiny bedroom for hours, with the stench of human excreta in her nostrils. Seb had come for her on his tractor when labour was well advanced, offering her a ride to his cottage. Fearing that she wouldn't arrive in time, what with this being Mrs Benson's sixth pregnancy, Maudie had left her bicycle at home and travelled in state, perched on the step of the ancient tractor.

The walk home was less than a mile, but Maudie was only halfway home when she suddenly felt extremely weary. All she wanted was to get indoors, have a quick bath and a cup of cocoa, and then have an early night. The graveyard stretched off to her left, its ancient yews casting dark shadows in the moonlight. The thought of trudging all the way round its perimeters suddenly became too much. If she nipped across the graveyard she could cut off a good couple of hundred yards. She hesitated.

Maudie did not believe in ghosts, nor did she fear the dead. The place seemed eerie enough at night but there was really nothing to fear. The sexton kept the gravel paths well raked, and she was in no danger of bumping into a tombstone. In the distance a solitary light shone out from what must be a bedroom in the rectory, and Maudie surmised that the Blunts were also planning an early night. Coming to a decision, she felt for the latch on the heavy iron gate and stepped inside the cemetery.

Somewhere nearby an owl hooted, and there was a rustling in the grass that spoke of some small animal hunting for prey. Maudie stopped to listen, drinking in the night air. A sudden pain in her foot caused her to curse softly. Old Pratt had done his work too well and a loose piece of gravel had somehow found its way into her shoe. She was not about to hobble all the way home with what felt like a chunk of the Rock of Gibraltar beneath her heel. Annoyed, she bent over to deal with it.

Before she realized what was happening, a savage blow to the hips knocked her off balance and she fell to the path, with a heavy body on top of her. Unable to wriggle free she managed to scream, and once started she was unable to stop. At at once the graveyard seemed full of people. She could just make out the figures of two men struggling on the verge, and even as she watched in horror she felt a pat on the back, which made her recoil.

'It's all right, Nurse! Matt's got him on the run.' Maudie recognized the voice of young Greta Black, the pregnant teenager whose progress she was monitoring.

Now she saw the vicar hurrying towards them, carrying a lighted lantern in his hand. 'What's going on here?' he demanded. 'What's happening?'

Mrs Blunt joined them. Maudie noted that the vicar's wife wore a floral cotton dressing gown, with her head a mass of curlers.

'He's got away!' Matt panted, addressing the vicar. 'But I know who he is. It's that rep chap that's staying at the Royal Oak.'

'Are you sure?' Maudie said. 'He left long ago.'

'I don't know about that, but he's back now, and he was out to get you, miss.'

'Inside, all of you!' the vicar snapped. 'I'll give Dick Bryant a ring, and no doubt he'll want to speak to all of us.'

Lying on a worn sofa in the rectory, Maudie suddenly realized that she was wide awake, with no trace of her earlier fatigue.

'What I'd like to know is, what were all of you doing in the graveyard at this time of night?' Mr Blunt said sternly. The clock on the mantelpiece struck nine as he said this, but nobody suggested that it really wasn't that late.

'I've been with Muriel Black,' Maudie said. 'Another little boy and both are well.'

'Very nice,' the vicar said. 'And what about you two?'

Greta blushed and said nothing. It was

obvious to Maudie what the pair of them had been up to, but she was only too glad that they'd been there when they were needed. She explained this to Dick Bryant when he arrived.

'I take it you struggled, and managed to wrestle the fellow to the ground?' he asked. 'Or did Matt here pounce in the nick of time?'

'I didn't hear him coming,' Maudie said, shuddering at the thought. 'The moon went behind a cloud just then. He must have been about to grab me by the throat' — she gulped — 'but just as he sprang I bent down to remove a stone from my shoe and he must have fallen over me.'

Mrs Blunt murmured something about a guardian angel. 'You must stay here tonight, Nurse. I can't have you going back to your own cottage with that maniac on the loose.'

'We'll soon have him in custody,' Bryant said, 'but yes, I agree that you should stay here, Nurse. You've had a bad shock.'

Maudie stared at him piteously, a sight that melted his heart. As she struggled to sit up he bent over and swept her into a bear hug. 'I really couldn't bear it if anything happened to you,' he whispered into her ear.

Before she could respond he released her and turned to Greta. 'As for you, young woman,' he said, 'you get off home right away, and mind you see her to the door, Matt Flynn! Nobody is safe until we get this Smith behind bars. That's if you're quite sure it was him.'

'Of course it was,' Matt said. 'I've seen him about the place, haven't I?'

25

'I'll lend you one of my nightgowns,' Mrs Blunt told Maudie. 'I could ask Harold to take you to your cottage to fetch one of your own but as he was already in bed and asleep before this happened . . . '

'Thank you very much,' Maudie told her. 'Are you sure it's convenient for me to stay? I'd probably be all right at home with all the doors and windows locked.'

'I wouldn't hear of your going home after what you've been through, and neither would Harold. I'm going to play nurse and put you to bed with a mug of Horlicks and a couple of Aspro. The bed in the spare room is already made up, so I'll just slip a hot water bottle in while you're getting ready. Would you perhaps fancy a bath? I think there's enough hot water.'

'I'd just like to get into bed, Mrs Blunt, and pull the covers over my head, if you don't mind.'

'Very well, but not until you take that hot drink to settle your stomach.' The vicar's wife produced a cellophane strip of Aspro and tore off two tablets, which she handed to Maudie.

Later, in spite of the hot water bottle that she clutched to her stomach, Maudie felt waves of cold breaking over her. She longed for her woolly bed socks but had to make do with a towel wrapped round her feet instead. The door creaked and she jerked upright in fright, but moments later a furry body landed on her legs and she realized that it was Perkin, the Blunts' ginger tom. She reached out for him gratefully and he settled down beside her, purring like a little engine.

She heard the church clock strike ten, then eleven and twelve. She couldn't help thinking about Dick Bryant. She had felt so safe and warm, held in his embrace for that brief moment. She could still feel the butterfly kiss he'd placed on her hair before releasing her. Or had she imagined that? Her nasty experience in the churchyard might be playing havoc with her mind. She must have fallen asleep at last, for the next thing she knew Mrs Blunt was standing beside her, holding a cup of tea, and the room was flooded with daylight.

'I hesitated to disturb you, Nurse, but not knowing your plans for the day I thought it best to wake you. Did I do right?'

'What's the time?'

'Gone seven. And there's a bit of news you'll be glad to hear. Dick Bryant called round a little while ago and they've got Smith in custody.'

Maudie began to shake. Mrs Blunt set the cup and saucer down on bedside table and gathered her friend into her arms. 'There, there! You're having a bit of a delayed reaction, I expect. I shouldn't have sprung the news on you so abruptly.'

'No, no! Believe me, I'm thankful to know that they've caught up with the beastly man. I mean, what might he have done next?'

'All's well that ends well,' Mrs Blunt said, 'although not for poor Cyril Swain, of course. Now then, what would you like for breakfast? We're having kedgeree, or I could do you a boiled egg if you prefer.'

Maudie swung her legs over the side of the bed, reaching for her tea. 'I think if you don't mind I'll pop home and have something there. I need a clean uniform in any case. Do you mind?'

'If you're sure you feel up to it, Nurse.' Mrs Blunt smiled. 'Come along, Perkin, you silly old cat. There's a nice bit of fish in the kitchen for you. It didn't all go into the kedgeree!' The cat followed her out, holding his tail upright in a furry question mark.

* * *

Maudie was sitting in her office, trying to make order out of the chaos of her scattered records, when the constable arrived.

'All present and correct, Nurse?' he asked, smiling.

'Oh, I'm a tough old bird,' Maudie assured him. 'You can't keep a Rouse down for long!'

'That's good to know.'

'I hear you've caught up with that dratted Smith.'

'We did, yes, but it was touch and go. It was a bit of luck that young Matt recognized him because I was able to get straight over to the Royal Oak before he had a chance to get away. I guessed he'd want to collect his bits and pieces from his room there, and of course his car was sitting there in the yard, ready for him to make a quick getaway. I took the precaution of letting the air out of his tyres before I went in and nabbed him.'

'That was quick thinking,' Maudie said approvingly.

'That's what Sarge said. Of course I can't claim all the glory. Len Frost helped me get the chap under control. Gave him a sock on the jaw to fell him, and sat on his chest while I got the handcuffs on him.'

'Fancy!'

'The inspector's coming over from Midvale this morning and he'll see what the chap has to say for himself, but it seems pretty obvious that this Smith is responsible for all the attacks round here, beginning with the murder of Cyril Swain. He'll hang, Nurse; I'm sure of it.'

'That's all very well,' Maudie said, 'but what I want to know is, why? All right, so he caught me snooping, but what about poor Miss Plummer? And why did Mr Swain have to die?'

Bryant shrugged. 'Perhaps he's a loony, Nurse. He may not have had any particular reason for doing what he did. If we hadn't caught him he might have carried on bumping off innocent people. You nipping through the churchyard and getting pounced on the way you did was a piece of luck for us, Nurse!'

'Oh, thank you very much, Dick Bryant!' Maudie roared. 'I'm so glad I was able to give you the break you needed, even if it did almost cost me my life! And haven't I been saying all along there was something fishy about the man? But did anybody listen? No!'

'I'll ignore the sarcasm,' Bryant told her, grinning. 'I'm sorry you had such a fright, but you've come to no harm, have you?'

'I suppose not.'

'That's all right, then. Well, I must be off. Don't be surprised if the inspector comes calling. He'll probably want a word with you. So long!'

'TTFN!' Maudie replied. Neither of them had referred to the tender little moment in the rectory sitting room. For Maudie it held a dreamlike quality now.

Detective Inspector Parry was Welsh, a middle-aged man with black hair and eyes. He was pleasant enough to Maudie, but there was something about him that told her he could be very harsh indeed when dealing with anyone who found himself on the wrong side of the law. Rather than sitting in the cramped conditions of her small office, she had elected to meet with the two officers in her own home, where she could relax in her favourite armchair.

'Do you make a habit of walking through the churchyard at night, Miss Rouse?' Parry asked. 'There's not many ladies who would fancy that.'

'Well no, I don't, as a matter of fact. It's just that I was exhausted after a heavy day and I couldn't wait to get home and put my feet up. I couldn't face going the long way round when cutting through the graveyard saves a few hundred yards.'

Parry looked at her, his face expressionless. 'Then how could Smith have expected to find you there, and at that time of evening?'

Maudie's hand went to her mouth. 'You mean he's been following me about,' she said. 'Stalking me.' The idea that Smith had been creeping along behind her, for goodness knew how long, was terrifying. She gulped. 'I suppose I should have known better. I just didn't think.'

'Then let's have a think now, shall we? Why do you think he wanted to attack you? We won't use the word kill, because according to him he only wanted to frighten you off, if you can believe that. What exactly have you done to bring that on yourself? Oh, Bryant here has filled me in, but I'd like to hear the story in your own words, please, Miss Rouse.'

Maudie hesitated while she arranged her thoughts in order. 'As you probably know, it was me who found poor Mr Swain's body. Naturally I've been wondering ever since who was responsible, and people have had all sorts of theories.

The only thing they all had in common is that some stranger must have done it.'

'Go on.'

'I know that people want to believe that some outsider was responsible rather than one of our own, but this is a small community and if one of the locals did it I'm sure they'd have been found out by now. I travel all over a wide area in my work, so I've kept my eyes open for any strangers, and this John Smith seemed to fit the bill.'

'Why was that? Feminine intuition, perhaps?'

Maudie hung her head, feeling foolish. 'I don't know. I just didn't take to the chap, I suppose.' Parry raised his eyebrows.

'Call it what you like,' she blurted, 'but I was right, wasn't I? And I have the grazed knees to prove it!'

'It looks as if you were, Miss Rouse, for as soon as we got him in the interview room he confessed to killing Swain. It takes some of them like that; after bottling it all up for so long they have to let it all spill out.'

'And did he say why?' Maudie asked, but Parry shook his head at her.

'We're in the middle of a police investigation, Miss Rouse, and I can't say more. I thank you for your help, and we may need to speak to you again later.'

Maudie ushered them to the door, feeling vaguely unsatisfied.

26

'Nurse! Nurse!' Maudie braked suddenly, putting one foot to the ground. She was surprised to see Bob Willis racing down his farm lane, waving vigorously at her. She leaned her bicycle against the gatepost and waited for him to reach her.

'You've got to come!' he panted. 'I've never seen anything like it!'

'What's up, Mr Willis? Is it one of the little girls?'

'No, it's the wife. She's taking on something awful, sobbing and throwing herself about. She'll do herself an injury if she keeps on like that. Real hysterical, she is. I've slapped her face but it didn't do no good.'

Maudie frowned. Slapping the face of a hysterical person might be the accepted treatment but she had never approved of it. There were other ways of delivering a sudden, sharp shock to divert the victim's attention without delivering physical violence.

'Calm down, man. Let me deal with this, hmm? You go about your work while I see what's going on. I'll call you if I need you. Where is Mrs Willis now? In the house?'

He nodded. 'In the kitchen, Nurse. I saw you on the road so I came running, otherwise I wouldn't have come out. She's not fit to be left!'

Maudie hoped that his wife hadn't suffered a miscarriage. It would be too bad if she had fallen pregnant with the longed-for baby, only to lose it in the early weeks. And if she had, it would be tenderness and sympathy she was in need off, not a slap on the cheek, poor soul! Unfortunately most men had no idea of the emotional pain that accompanied the loss of a baby, believing that it could easily be replaced and therefore need not be mourned.

Maudie found Mrs Willis perched on a kitchen chair, rocking herself back and forth with her apron thrown over her head. She looked like a woman who had encountered something too awful to be faced. Maudie had seen many such scenes in London during the blitz; the human spirit can only take so much before retreating from reality. Turning to the husband, who was hovering in the doorway, she waved him away and firmly closed the door.

'Mrs Willis!' she said gently. 'Can you hear me, Mrs Willis? It's Nurse Rouse, come to see if I can help.'

The distraught woman slowly lowered her floral apron and sat up, revealing a tear-stained face. 'Oh, Nurse,' she shuddered. 'Where have you sprung from? I didn't send for you.'

'Your husband saw me passing by,' Maudie said gently. 'He thought you might need someone to talk to.'

Tears welled up in the soft brown eyes. 'I've been worried for so long. I didn't know what to do for the best, so I just did nothing. Now they've caught that chap I see I was wrong all along, and my Bob is in the clear.'

Bob Willis, in the clear? Maudie was puzzled. 'You'd better tell me all about it, get it off your chest,' she said. 'You know what they say: a worry shared is a worry halved. But first, you give your face and hands a lick and promise while I put the kettle on. This calls for a cup of tea.'

When Maudie judged that the other woman was in a fit state to talk, she leaned across the table to squeeze her hand. 'Right, then! You've been worried about your man. You seemed to be afraid he'd been up to something. What was that? Another woman? Dealing on the black market? You can tell me, Mrs Willis. It won't go any further, unless you give me permission.'

Mrs Willis sniffed. 'You remember that Mr Swain that was murdered?'

Maudie coughed. 'I could hardly forget him, seeing that it was me that found the poor chap.'

'So you did, Nurse. So you did. I was forgetting that. Well, I thought it was my Bob that killed him, see?'

Maudie was left speechless for a long moment. 'But why?' she asked. 'Mr Swain was a visitor to the area. How did your husband even know the man?'

'Because he came here, asking about our Polly. He was her grandfather, Swain was.'

'What!'

Mrs Willis sighed. 'I suppose you'll have to know. Polly isn't Bob's child. Early on in the war I met this chap in the Air Force and we fell in love. A bomber pilot, he was. When he heard I was in the family way he promised to do the right thing by me. We planned to get wed but he was killed on the very first raid he went on, shot down over the Channel. Well, you know what it was like in those days, Nurse. I was in a real fix and I didn't know how I was going to manage once the baby arrived. Then I met Bob. He used to deliver vegetables to the shop where I worked, and he'd asked me out once or twice. When he heard about my trouble he offered to marry me and I jumped at the chance.'

'I see.'

'Then we came here and I thought it would turn out for the best. Everyone would assume that Polly is Bob's child and she'd grow up being none the wiser. We expected that little brothers and sisters would come along for her in due course, but it's never happened. Bob knows it can't be my fault, not with me having Polly to show for it, so it must be him who can't father kids. It's been preying on his mind something awful, Nurse, and he does get ratty at times.'

'But Mr Swain,' Maudie prompted. 'Where does he come into the picture?'

'He turned up here one day completely out of the blue, saying he was Teddy's father. That was my chap, see, Edward Swain. He must have told his parents there was a baby coming, and we were meaning to tie the knot. Teddy was their only child, and Mr Swain promised his wife he'd find their grandchild somehow, so she could get to know Teddy's little boy or girl before she died. She's not well and they've got her in a home somewhere, down in Devonshire.'

'He left it a bit late,' Maudie said, 'seeing that your Polly is seven years old now.'

Mrs Willis produced a sodden handkerchief from her apron pocket and dabbed at her eyes.

'But we moved, don't forget, and they didn't know of me as Willis. My name was Patterson when Teddy knew me. By what his dad said, they'd had to put a private eye on the case before they found me.'

'Patterson!' Maudie exclaimed. 'Someone over in Brookfield told me he was hunting for a Nellie Patterson. But your name is . . . '

'Helen, but Nellie was Teddy's pet name for me. My little Nell, he used to call me, after some character in a book he liked to read, by Charles Dickens, I think it was.'

Helen Willis had a faraway look on her face and seemed disinclined to go on with her story. Remembering happier days, Maudie supposed. But they hadn't yet reached the heart of the story, and she was eager to hear more.

'So Swain came here, did he?'

Mrs Willis blinked several times before answering. 'He turned up here one Monday morning. I remember that, clear as clear, because it was washday and I was putting sheets through the mangle when this knock came at the door. This man was standing on the doorstep

— Cyril Swain, as it turned out. I thought at first he was selling something, and I was all set to send him away with a flea in his ear, but he told me he was Teddy's dad, and that got me all of a tizzy. I had to let him in then, of course, though I've regretted it since.'

'And he asked to see Polly?'

'Yes, but she was at school. He wanted a photo to take back to his wife but we didn't have one. Then he asked if he could come back later to meet her, and that's when Bob came in. I've never seen him so worked up, Nurse. He said we wanted nothing to do with these Swains, thank you very much. He shouted at Mr Swain to clear off and never come back, and if he ever tried to contact us again he'd kill him.'

Maudie could understand why, in a way. Learning the truth could upset Polly and it would expose Helen's pathetic little secret. Worst of all, in Bob's eyes, he'd be branded as a husband who couldn't father children — a sad reflection on his manhood. 'And did the old chap leave when he was told to?' she asked.

Mrs Willis nodded. 'Yes, but he didn't go quietly. He'd be back, he said, even if he had to bring a policeman with him. As the child's grandfather he had rights, and he owed it to his dead son to show Polly to his wife. Bob shoved him out of the door and I never saw the chap again. I hoped that was the end of it.'

'Until Polly went missing,' Maudie murmured.

'We thought Swain must have taken her,' Mrs Willis agreed, getting up and pacing around the kitchen.

'But she was returned safely, and then Swain died.'

'Yes, and I thought that Bob had killed him. All the time he kept shouting that he'd have to get rid of the chap if he wouldn't leave us alone, and then you found that poor man dead, Nurse. What would you have thought if you were me?'

27

'You might have asked him,' Maudie said sternly.

Helen Willis stared at her as if she were mad. 'If you can say that, Nurse, then you don't know my hubby! He's got a temper on him, has Bob, though he simmers down quick enough after he blows up. If I'd asked a fool question like that I might not be here to tell the tale.'

'In which case you probably didn't ask because you were afraid of the answer you might get,' Maudie remarked, realizing as she spoke that her words could be taken two ways.

The other woman heaved a sigh. For a moment Maudie thought she was about to cry again, but she pulled herself together and looked Maudie in the eye.

'I don't want to think that my husband is a killer, but look at the facts. Swain doesn't come from these parts, but he arrives here looking for me, saying he wants to get to know our Polly. The next thing we know she's disappeared, most likely kidnapped by him. I mean, what else were we to think? Then she came back but she hasn't said a word from that day to this, so we're no closer to knowing what really happened. Then Swain is killed. Bob's been going round like a bear with a sore head ever since, and I've been climbing the walls, imagining all sorts. I tell you, Nurse, it's a wonder I haven't gone stark, staring mad!'

'You really should have told all this to Dick Bryant,' Maudie said, but in Helen's place wouldn't she have done the same to protect her husband? 'Listen to me,' she went on, 'you need to come forward now, my dear. They've got that Smith fellow in custody, and it won't just be Dick Bryant on the case now. They've brought in the bigwigs from Midvale to question him and who knows what he'll come out with? They'll be at your door before you know it. If you take my advice you'll go and see Dick before you're another day older, and tell him what you know. If you don't, then I shall be forced to stick my oar in. I could get into trouble for withholding vital evidence, and so will you.'

'I'll think about it,' Mrs Willis said, but judging by the stubborn expression on the woman's face, Maudie wasn't sure that she would co-operate.

* * *

All this excitement set Maudie back a good half hour and she was all behind with her home visits. Not that anyone seemed to mind. They were all agog to know about the capture of John Smith, assuming that Maudie would be fully in the picture, which she was not.

'They must have told you summat,' Daisy Larke's father grumbled when she called at their cottage to check on baby Richard. 'Why did he throttle old Swain, then? How did he come to know him in the first place? And what was he doing having a go at you, Nurse, and that poor young teacher, eh? What harm did she ever do to anyone?'

'I don't know about little Miss Plummer,' Maudie told him, 'but I reckon he wanted to shut me up because I was getting too close for comfort.'

'How's that, then?'

'I've been asking too many questions, I suppose.'

Fred screwed up his face in a horrible grimace. 'A prattling woman and a cackling hen, ain't no good to beast nor men,' he quoted.

'Dad!' Daisy hissed, but the old man merely nodded and started to draw on his pipe.

Pink-cheeked, Maudie could find no words of rebuttal. She longed to share the information she had garnered at the Willis farm but she felt she owed it to them to keep quiet, at least for a while. She'd give the woman a day or two to own up to the police and then she'd have to come forward herself. In the meantime it would be wicked to add fuel to the gossip that was going around the district like a forest fire after a thunderstorm.

'They were saying at the mothers' meeting that it must have been Smith who kidnapped young Polly Willis,' Daisy said, her eyes bright with excitement.

'What do you think, Nurse? Can that be right?'

'We don't actually know if she was kidnapped,' Maudie pointed out. 'And until she starts speaking again we won't know what took place, if then. The doctor thinks she may have been in trouble at home and went into hiding to avoid punishment, or to pay them out. 'I'll make them think I'm dead and then they'll be sorry.' That sort of thing.'

'Rubbish!' the old man said. 'It's obvious, ain't it? That Smith is one of them perverts, what likes to take advantage of little girls. He got his filthy hands on her and that's why she's not talking. Too frightened, ain't she? Stands to reason!'

'I can assure you, Mr Miller, that Polly wasn't harmed in any way. She was tired and hungry, but nothing worse; and since I was the first to examine her, I can vouch for the truth of that.'

He wasn't convinced. 'He must've been frightened off before he could do anything, like he was when he tried it on with the school teacher. Mind you, I put my money on that Cox fellow at the time and I could be proved right yet, for now she's out of the way he's walked into her job, hasn't he? Something fishy about that if you ask me.'

'Do you think there's two of them then, Dad?' Daisy asked. 'This Smith killed Cyril Swain, and someone else tried to do for Emma Plummer?'

'Aye, gal. Could be, could be.'

'Aren't you forgetting something?' Maudie said coldly. 'Smith tried to finish me off, too!'

'Just putting the frighteners on you I reckon,' Fred said, shrugging.

'It felt like more than that to me,' Maudie said, remembering back to her experience in the churchyard. She hoped that all these little puzzles would be solved eventually, although she knew from experience that life's mysteries were seldom unraveled to one's complete satisfaction. However, there was always hope. Smith had already confessed to killing Cyril Swain, so why should he hold back from explaining the other facets of the crime? After all they could only hang him once, and he might be glad to get things off his conscience, if in fact he had one.

A loud wailing made them all jump. 'That's our Richard off again,' Daisy said. 'Sounds like he wants changing. He's had a bit of nappy rash and that's made him grumpy. I've done my best not to let him lie there in a wet nappy but I think he needs something to put on his bottom, if you can suggest anything that would work. Do you want to look at him now, Nurse?'

'Next time I'm passing this way I'll let you have some zinc ointment to put on it, Daisy. In the meantime you can dust his little bottom with corn flour. That should help. And if we do happen to get a warm day, let him lie in the sun for a little while without his nappy.'

Little Richard's mouth curved in a smile when he recognized his mother bending over his cot, and he raised his arms to her, expecting to be picked up. Daisy reached for her son, beaming down at him as if he was the most precious treasure on earth. Watching the two of them together, Maudie felt a wave of peace breaking over her. Working with mothers and babies was the best job on earth, and she wouldn't change her occupation for the world.

It was all very well playing at being Miss Marple, she thought, as she pedalled her way home that afternoon, but all this crime and passion was getting to be too much for her. She longed for a return to the days when a little boy's nappy rash was the only cloud on the horizon.

28

'Miss! Miss!' Riding past the school, cycling slowly in case one of the children should dash out unexpectedly, Maudie saw Lily Willis clinging to the iron railings, hopping from one foot to the other in her excitement.

Dismounting carefully, Maudie propped her machine against a convenient lamp-post and approached the child. She hoped this wasn't about to be another discussion about where babies come from as she had a full agenda of home visits on which she was eager to get started.

'Polly wants to tell you something,' Lily whispered. Maudie noticed Polly Willis hovering in the background, half hidden by a small group of girls who were taking turns skipping under a long rope, wielded by two of their number and chanting:

'Nebuchadnezzar, king of the Jews
Sold his wife for a pair of shoes
But when the shoes began to wear

Nebuchadnezzar began to swear . . . '

'Polly wants to tell me something?' she queried. 'Do you mean she's found her voice again?'

Lily shook her head. 'She'll tell me and I can tell you,' she murmured.

'All right, Lily. Let's get on with it then, shall we? I've a lot to do today.'

Lily turned and waved to Polly, who slowly came forward with a wary look in her eye. She whispered something in her foster sister's ear.

'She said it was the bad man,' Lily reported.

'Bad man? Who was that, then?'

'You know, the one what they took away in the Black Miler.'

'Black Miler? What on earth?' Suddenly, light dawned. 'Do you mean the police van, the Black Maria?' Both girls nodded vigorously. John Smith, then! Go carefully, Maudie Rouse! If you don't spook this pair you may learn something to your advantage.

'So you saw the police taking a man away, did you? I expect they wanted to talk to him about something, didn't they?'

Polly punched her sister on the arm. Lily turned back to Maudie. 'It was him, silly. The man what stole Polly away!'

Maudie felt her heart flutter in her breast. 'Oh, yes?'

'She didn't take any sweeties,' Lily said fearfully. Polly shook her head from side to side to emphasize this.

'Of course she didn't,' Maudie assured them. 'Mummy has told you never to take sweeties from strangers, I expect.'

'And Miss Plummer and Miss Rice!'

'But Polly went somewhere with the man, did she?' (Easy, Maudie! Don't frighten them off.)

'His dog was lost. The man wanted Polly to help find it, cos it's just a puppy and it would be so frightened all by itself.'

A great rage welled up in Maudie. Was there no end to the tricks that evil men would get up to in order to lure unsuspecting children away? Offering sweets was seldom any good because they'd all been warned against that, but what child could resist a sob story about a lost puppy? She reminded herself that Polly hadn't been abused, but whatever had taken place was enough to make her lose the power of speech for all these weeks.

'Did you find the lost puppy, Polly?' The girl shook her head again and leaned into Lily's shoulder, whispering something in her ear.

'He said he'd take her to see a kangaroo,' Lily reported.

'A kangaroo? He was going to the zoo, was he?'

'No, Miss. he was going to Orse . . . Orse . . . that place where kangaroos live.'

'Do you mean Australia?' Both girls nodded.

'Well, that was silly, wasn't it?' Maudie said, managing a laugh. 'Australia is a long, long way away. You wouldn't want to go so far away from mummy and daddy, would you? And never mind about the kangaroo! Perhaps Daddy will take you to the zoo one of these days, and you can see one there.'

Miss Rice emerged from the school, ringing a hand bell. 'Gotta go!' Lily said.

Maudie wanted to know more. Polly

seemed willing to confide in Lily now, but it would be too bad if she clammed up again before they got to the bottom of this business.

'Hang on a minute, girls. There's something else I have to ask. Miss Rice won't mind, when she knows you're with me. Polly, how did you get away from the man?'

'Her granddad saw the man and told him to leave go,' Lily said.

'Do you mean Mr Swain, Polly?' But Polly looked at her blankly. Maudie was dying to ask more questions but something told her she'd gone far enough.

Miss Rice came out of the door again, beckoning imperiously to the two children, who scampered off. Maudie was left alone on the other side of the railings, her mind in a whirl.

* * *

'Nurse! Nurse! Can I have a word?' She came to with a start. A young man dressed in an ancient suit and shabby boots was crossing the street towards her.

'Mick Sawyer,' he said, first extending a grubby hand before withdrawing it hastily and wiping it on the seat of his pants.

'What can I do for you, Mr Sawyer?'

'Our Patsy told me she met you the other day, Nurse.'

'Oh, yes, so she did. How can I help?'

'She's expecting our first, is Patsy,' he said proudly.

'So I noticed.'

'Yes, well, I want to know if you'll take her on. See to her, like, when her time comes.'

'Well of course I'd be glad to,' Maudie said, 'but I understood your wife to say that her grandmother will be in charge.'

'Oh, her! She's got some funny ideas, does Nan Bentley. She puts a needle on a bit of thread and waves it over our Patsy's stomach, like. Says she can tell that way if the baby's going to be a boy or a girl. Silly old trout.'

'I don't see much harm in that,' Maudie told him. The countryside was full of old superstitions like that and fifty percent of the time the predictions were correct!

'Maybe not, but she won't be bringing my son into the world. She's fallen over and busted her hip. Going to be in hospital for fourteen weeks, the doctor said, trussed up like a turkey ready for the roasting pan. That's if she comes out at all, at her age.'

'I'm sorry to hear that,' Maudie said, meaning it. 'You ask your wife to pop into my office tomorrow morning and we'll discuss the details. I shall want to advise her on diet,' she added, recalling the sight of young Mrs Sawyer filling her face with cream cakes.

'Oh, you don't have to worry about our Patsy, Nurse. She has a big fry-up every morning now she's stopped feeling sick. She loves a bit of fried bread plastered with dripping, does Patsy.'

'Imagine!' Maudie said faintly.

That settled, she continued on her rounds, but when at the end of the day she was passing the Willis home she decided to call in. Helen Willis looked at her in alarm.

'There's noting wrong, is there, Nurse? You haven't come to tell me something's happened to my Bob?'

'No, Mrs Willis. In fact, it's good news in a way. I've discovered that your Polly has started to talk again. At least, not directly, but she whispers things to Lily, who has become her mouthpiece.'

Helen's mouth widened into a big smile. 'Thank goodness! Oh, I am pleased! I'll have a few words to say to that girl when she gets home, keeping us in the dark all this time!'

'I do think you should be cautious, Mrs Willis, until we know the whole story. Perhaps if you let her communicate with you through Lily?'

'I suppose I could, Nurse, but what did you find out?'

'Not a great deal, except that it was Smith who lured her away.'

'Haven't I told those girls never to take sweets from strangers?' Helen cried. 'I've told them and told them, and now see what happens!'

'It seems that he spun Polly a yarn about a lost puppy, and then he promised to take her to Australia to see a kangaroo.'

Helen shook her head in disbelief.

'Australia! Where on earth would he get an idea like that? And if he did mean to take her away from here, what did he want with her? When I think of what could have happened . . . ' Suddenly overcome, she began to sob.

'Buck up, dear,' Maudie said. 'It's pointless fretting over something that never happened. There is one thing I'd like to know, though; Lily seems to be implying that it was her grandfather who saved her from Smith's clutches. Could that have been Cyril Swain?'

29

After wrestling with her conscience, Maudie telephoned Dick Bryant, who said he'd come to see her immediately.

'Are you calling from home, or the office?' he asked.

'I'm at home now, but I'll see you at the office,' she told him.

'Right ho!'

Maudie sat back, relieved. She had thought twice about contacting him because Helen Willis had told her certain things in confidence. However, her encounter with the little girls, and the strange tale they'd shared with her, was something she felt bound to report. She wasn't sure what it was all about, but the information might help the police enquiry. It would be dreadful if Smith were let off for lack of sufficient evidence.

'Right, then,' Bryant said, removing his uniform helmet and placing it on her desk. 'You say that Polly Willis is talking now? Why hasn't her mother let us know?'

'You can ask her that yourself,' Maudie said, trying to be diplomatic. She had no wish to drop Helen in it, but hadn't she told the woman to contact the police? It was hardly Maudie's fault if she'd failed to do so. 'All I know is what the children said to me, and how much of it is true and how much is fantasy I really can't say. Children have vivid imaginations, you know.'

'Suppose you start at the beginning, Nurse. Where did this conversation take place?'

'At the school. I was passing by when little Lily called out to me.'

'Lily! That's the other child. I thought you said it was Polly who spoke to you.'

'Not directly. She kept whispering in Lily's ear, and then Lily reported her words to me.'

Bryant scratched his forehead. 'I don't know, Nurse. Do you suppose the kiddie was making it up, to draw attention to herself? Young Polly has been made much of ever since her disappearance, and Lily may be feeling left out.'

'I didn't get that impression. If anybody is making things up I'd say it was Polly.'

'Go on.'

'Polly insists that Smith, or 'the bad man' as she calls him, was the person who lured her away. Both children insist that they didn't accept sweets from him, nor were any offered. Apparently he spun Polly a yarn about a lost puppy and she went with him quite willingly to help him search for the creature.'

'Bastard!'

'Quite! He then told her he would take her to Australia, to show her a kangaroo.'

'I wonder why he picked Australia?' Bryant said thoughtfully. 'We'll have to ask him about that.'

'There's something else. The child says she was able to get free of him because her granddad intervened.'

'Granddad? Who would that be, then?'

Maudie played her trump card. 'Cyril Swain, Constable. He was Polly's grandfather!'

'What! Do you know this for a fact?'

She nodded. 'That's what he was doing

in the area. He'd come here in the hope of locating the child. Polly is the daughter of Helen Willis, as she is now, and Swain's son, who was killed in action during the war.'

Bryant frowned. 'I hope I don't have to charge you with withholding vital information in a police investigation, Nurse! If there is anything else you haven't told me, for goodness' sake spit it out now!'

'I suggest you have a chat with Helen Willis,' Maudie said, trying to look innocent. 'I have no way of knowing the truth of that story, which is why I've not said anything before. I'm not one to spread malicious gossip, Constable. I've a job to do in this area and I wouldn't get very far if my patients thought of me as a blabbermouth.'

'But you are sure that's what the child said? That her grandfather, whom you believe to be Swain, was the one who rescued her from Smith?'

Maudie nodded. Bryant slammed his fist down on her desk. 'There are more holes in this story than my mother's colander, Nurse!'

'Well, you can hardly blame me for that,' she muttered, alarmed by the violence of his gesture.

'Sorry if I startled you,' he said, grinning ruefully. 'I was just thinking aloud. Of course I don't blame you, Nurse. I just get so upset when I hear about kiddies falling into the clutches of swine like Smith. It seems odd to me that, having rescued his little granddaughter, Swain didn't take her straight home to her mother. Why was that? And where was she all the time she was missing?'

'And I'd like to know what that beastly man meant to do with the child! Do you think there was anything in that Australia business?'

'I don't know, but I'm jolly well going to find out. I expect it was just another come-on, though. There was no puppy and Polly probably tried to get away from him, telling him she wanted to go home. We don't know where he was keeping her, but no doubt he wanted to stop her making a fuss, so he promised her the kangaroo. A child of that age doesn't have much grasp of distances. Australia could be just down the road for all she knows.' Maudie had a sudden and horrible mental picture of poor Cyril Swain, lying in the woods with his tongue hanging out. 'Why did Mr Swain have to die?' she asked.

'Isn't that obvious? The man knew what Smith had been up to, so he had to be killed to prevent him talking.'

'Sounds a bit extreme to me. Smith could have left the district and nobody would have thought twice about it. He's a rep, on the move all the time, going from one place to another. It was the perfect cover.'

'The job may have been the perfect cover for something else, you know. Let's suppose his purpose in coming here was to snatch the child. He lays his plans carefully. He stops at the Royal Oak a couple of times, establishing his right to be there. Then, when the time is right, he pounces.'

Maudie stared at Bryant. 'But I thought your people had checked into his background and he turns out to be a bona fide rep for some company.'

'True enough.'

'Are you trying to tell me that this man got himself a job as a rep in order to come to Llandyfan to stalk Polly? That is so far-fetched! How could he have even known she existed, let alone make plans to kidnap her? It was Swain who had the motive for that, if anyone did.'

'I know,' Bryant groaned. 'I'm just letting my mind wander, in the hope of coming up with something. That's part of what they taught us at police college, Nurse. Use the scientific method.'

'Observation, reasoning and verification!' Maude chimed in. 'They told us that at nursing school, too!'

Bryant stood up, reaching down for his helmet. 'I must be on my way. Thanks for coming forward, Nurse.'

'You will have a word with Polly's mother, then?'

'No time like the present. I'm on my way there now, Nurse.'

When the door clicked for a second, time Maudie assumed that he'd forgotten to ask something and was coming back, but instead it was Mrs Blunt who entered. She was carrying a stack of Penguin paperbacks and she held out the pile to Maudie, beaming with pleasure.

'A parishioner just brought these in. He was having a clear-out and decided to donate them to the church, ready for the next jumble sale. Just look at all these green ones, Nurse.'

Maudie was well aware that the orange ones were for general fiction, while the green ones held crime and mystery. 'I have had enough mystery for one day, thank you!' she said, with a wry face.

'Dick Bryant gave you a grilling, did he? I saw him leaving just now. He seemed a bit bemused.'

'As well he might be,' Maudie said. 'I'm sure we'll never know the whole story, and that's what's driving me mad. I do hate not getting to the bottom of things, don't you?'

'I think I'll take this one for Harold,' Mrs Blunt said. *The Case of the Stuttering Bishop*, by Erle Stanley Gardner. Just up his alley, wouldn't you say?'

'I remember that,' Maudie said. 'They made a film of that before the war.'

'Did you see it? Was it any good?'

'I wanted to, but I happened to be studying for final exams right then and I didn't dare take the time off.'

'Never mind, you can read all about it now. Borrow it if you like and take it home with you.'

More to please Mrs Blunt than anything else, Maudie did take the book home, where she dipped into it while waiting for her potatoes to boil. Before she knew it she was hooked. It was about an Australian bishop who asks an American lawyer called Perry Mason to investigate the case of a woman who had been wrongfully accused of manslaughter two decades earlier.

Australia again! Were the guardian angels that were assigned to amateur sleuths trying to tell her something? Or had Smith merely settled on a kangaroo as something exotic enough to pique young Polly's interest?

30

'Thank goodness it's Saturday!' Maudie sighed. 'One way and another this has been a brute of a week, but now I'll have a few hours to myself. Such a relief!'

'What do you intend to do with them?' Mrs Blunt asked. They were sitting in the rectory kitchen, sipping coffee and exchanging news.

'I should wash a few things through, but I think I'll forget about that for now because I can't hang anything out to dry. Just look at that rain! It's teeming down, and I hate to have the house strewn with damp things, don't you? No, I think I'll dust around, make a few swipes with the carpet sweeper, and then I'll get back to Perry Mason!'

Mrs Blunt laughed. 'Weekends are our busy time here, of course. I look forward to Sunday evenings after Evensong when Harold and I sit down to do the crossword together. Do you know . . . '

But whatever she had been about to share with Maudie was interrupted by a tap at the door.

A plump young woman teetered on the step, smiling nervously.

'With fat knees like that she shouldn't wear such short skirts,' Maudie thought uncharitably, smugly conscious of her own shapely legs under her old tweed skirt.

'Yes; can I help you?' Mrs Blunt asked.

'Um, can I see the vicar, please?'

'Well no, I'm afraid you can't. He's out somewhere doing parish visits.'

The girl pouted. 'When will he be back?'

'I really can't say. One or two of his parishioners are bedridden and they do so like to chat. He doesn't like to rush them because he believes that his visits are the highlight of their week.'

'Fancy!'

'Would you care to make an appointment for another day?'

'I can't very well. This is my day off and I've come all the way from Midvale, see. Can't I wait here for him? I really need to see him today.'

'You'd better come in,' the vicar's wife said, standing aside to let her in. 'Do sit down. Now then, your name is . . . ?'

'Sally Evans. I'm the barmaid at the Spread Eagle in Midvale.'

'And you'd like to see my husband because . . . ?'

'To fix up about my wedding. I'm getting married and I want it here. It's such a pretty church.'

'St Dunstan's at Midvale is quite lovely,' Mrs Blunt remarked. 'Isn't that your parish church, my dear?'

'Oh, I don't really go to church,' her visitor said, crossing her legs and gazing admiringly at one high-heeled red shoe thus displayed. 'But your wedding's different, innit? It wants to be special, like.'

'Yes, indeed,' Mrs Blunt said. 'Well, I'm not sure what my husband would say. He might feel that St Dunstan's is more appropriate.'

'That's not what he'd think at all,' Maudie thought. She was quite familiar with the Reverend Harold Blunt's views on the subject. He was a devout man who believed that the church was an appropriate setting for similarly-minded couples to make their vows before God. It was not simply a backdrop to a social occasion.

'I was christened in St. John's,' the girl explained. 'My parents lived in these parts when I was a baby, only they moved away when my Dad lost his job and that's why you've never seen me before. That gives me some rights, don't it, me being christened here?'

'I'm sure that my husband will be able to answer your questions,' Mrs Blunt said, smiling. 'Now then, you've come a long way and the next bus won't be here for ages. Can I offer you a cup of tea, perhaps? Nurse and I were just having one.'

'I don't mind if I do, ta.' She stared at Maudie, who guessed what was coming next. 'You must be that nurse, the one who found the body.'

'I'm afraid so.'

'And is it true the killer tried to finish you off, and all?'

Maudie winced. 'It's true I was attacked by him, but I don't know, perhaps he just meant to frighten me off.'

The girl tossed her peroxided hair. 'Tell that to the Marines! I met both those chaps you know, the one who was murdered, and the one who done it.'

Maudie sat up straighter in her chair. 'No! Did you really?'

The girl nodded importantly. 'Like I said, I'm the barmaid at the Spread Eagle. I overheard the two of them talking, and later that night I had a bit of a fling with one of them, the one who said he was a rep, not the one who was killed.'

Mrs. Blunt's expression was bleak. 'What sort of a fling?'

'Oh, it's not what you're thinking, Mrs vicar's wife! I'm a good girl, I am. No, he bought me a couple of drinks and when I went off duty we went for a walk, that's all.'

'And what did your fiancé think of that?'

'Jim? Nothing to think about. I wasn't getting up to nothing. Just stringing the chap on a bit. This John Smith, he told me he knew where I could get nylons, off the ration, like. Well, I wanted to hear more about that, didn't I, seeing as I'm getting married and going on honeymoon to Bognor. Catch me wearing lisle stockings under my wedding dress!'

'I see.'

'And when he tried to kiss me I pushed him off and ran. In my line of work you get used to dealing with drunks.'

'You say you heard the two men talking,' Maudie murmured. 'Can you remember what they said?'

'Well, Smith was telling the other chap, whatsisname, how he was emigrating to Australia as soon as he'd finished a bit of business he had to do here.'

'Swain,' Maudie told her. 'The man who was murdered was called Cyril Swain.'

'Right-ho! Well, Swain, he asks did Smith think he was doing the right thing. A lot of people are emigrating these days but how do they know there'll be enough jobs to go round when they all get over there? Conditions could be worse than England on account of there being so many Australian servicemen going home after the war and wanting to settle down.

Oh, I'll be all right, Smith says. I have a sister over there and she'll put me up while I look around for work.'

'And then what?' Maudie prompted.

'We got busy then and I didn't hear no more. By the time the rush was over that Swain had gone again. That's when Smith started rabbiting on about them stockings, see.'

Maudie tried not to show her disappointment. 'Did Smith tell you anything more about himself while you were out walking?'

'Nothing that made any sense. You know what it's like when a chap's had one too many. Muttering and rambling on.'

'Think carefully, Miss Evans. Don't you realize that you went for a walk with a man who has killed once and may have attempted to kill again? Why, he might well have strangled you as well!'

The girl shrugged. 'But he hadn't killed anybody then, had he? I told you, old Swain was in the bar that night, alive and kicking.'

Maudie felt like strangling the girl herself. 'But he was murdered not long afterwards,' she pointed out. 'Don't you see, it's vital that we gather as much information as possible in the case against Smith, and if you know anything at all it could help solve a few puzzles connected with the case.'

Sally Evans curled her lip. 'Who do you think you are, then, Miss Marple?'

'No, just a plain old nurse who happened to discover a very real corpse. Are you sure there's nothing else you can tell us?'

'Well, I did look up once while I was serving, and it looked like them two was arguing. That Swain, he thumped his hand down on the table, shaking his head, and Smith clapped him on the back, like he was saying it was all right.'

'That what was all right?'

The girl shrugged. 'How should I know?'

Maudie felt like crying, so sure was she that the key to the whole mystery was somehow contained in that short meeting between the two men at the Spread Eagle. 'Have you reported this to the police?' she asked.

'What, and get done for dealing on the black market? Blow that for a lark!'

'But you didn't actually buy those stockings, did you?' Maudie pointed out, hoping she was right. 'We all wish there were more things available in the shops. There's no harm in talking about something like that. It doesn't mean that we go ahead and do something about it. No harm will come to you if you have a word with Dick Bryant or his superiors. You will do that, won't you, Miss Evans?'

'I might,' the girl said doubtfully. 'But don't you go saying nothing till I make up my mind, okay?'

31

Some days later Dick Bryant stepped into Maudie's little office, wearing a cheerful grin on his weather-beaten face.

'I thought you'd want to know the latest,' he said. 'The inspector is satisfied that it's all wrapped up nicely. Thanks in part to your help, all the ends have been tied up and Smith is on his way to London to face trial for the murder of Cyril Swain. The inspector is quite pleased and so am I. It should look well on my record.'

'Thank goodness for that! I've been so afraid he'd manage to weasel out of it somehow.'

'Understandable when he came after you before.'

'So what have you found out? Is there really a sister in Australia?'

'Yes. His sister is Ruth Martin, Lily's birth mother.'

Maudie's jaw dropped. 'But I thought

she was killed during the blitz!'

'Apparently not. Her mother's street was bombed, all right, and the old lady was killed, but Ruth wasn't home that night. I'm guessing that when the Home Guard came round asking questions they were told that two women had bought it in the bombed house, and with so much going on nobody bothered to check into it too deeply. This has been confirmed by Smith, who says that his sister found digs and a job somewhere, and just carried on as usual.'

'And where was he at the time?'

'In foreign parts, serving king and country, but the pair of them kept in touch by letter.'

'Did Helen Willis know about this? That Ruth had survived, I mean? Everyone here seems to think that Lily is an orphan.'

'Apparently not.'

'You mean to tell me that the woman just carried on as usual, without a thought for her little girl? I don't think much of that!'

Bryant shook his head. 'I think you're

forgetting, Nurse, that Lily was here as an evacuee. The woman would have assumed that the child was safe enough, and what would have been the point of taking the kiddie back to London? Thousands of women worked for the war effort in factories and the like and didn't see their children from one year's end to the other. That's what evacuation was all about.'

'Yes, but what sort of mother wouldn't send her children a card or a little gift for her birthday?' Even as she spoke, Maudie could see a possible explanation for that. During her nursing training days she had spent three months on the children's ward in a big hospital. Although some children had spent weeks there, recovering from operations, their parents hadn't been allowed to visit them. The prevailing wisdom of the time had been that the youngster would find it too unsettling when their mothers had to return home, leaving them behind. They would grieve and make a fuss and probably suffer a relapse that would affect their recovery.

'The war has been over for two years now,' she reminded him.

'Yes, well, she's been busy. She met an Australian bloke and married him and now she's gone with him to Doola Walla or wherever he calls home over there. She wants Lily back and she sent Smith to collect her. According to him she gave him a letter for the Willises, authorizing him to take the child away.'

'Sounds fishy to me! Why didn't she contact the Willises directly?'

'Don't ask me, Nurse! Perhaps she felt ashamed that she hadn't been in touch sooner. Meanwhile poor old Swain comes on the scene, looking for Polly. As I learned from Helen Willis — when she finally decided to confide in me — after managing to trace her he turns up at their home, claiming to be Polly's grandfather. Now Bob Willis is a jealous sort of customer and he didn't like to think of his wife's previous relationship with the child's father. The pair of them sent Swain away with a flea in his ear when he'd barely caught a glimpse of her.'

'This all sounds like too much of a coincidence to me,' Maudie said. 'I mean, what are the odds against two men turning up at the Willis place at the same time in search of the girls? And for that matter, how did Smith come to know Swain?'

'Coincidences do happen in life,' Bryant said, 'probably more often than we realize. As we know from the barmaid at the Spread Eagle the two men met there. Again, that may have been by chance; and possibly Swain, accepting Smith's cover story of being a rep, mentioned that he was trying to trace the grandchild he'd never met.

'This fits in with the rather incoherent tale Smith has to tell. Knowing that Helen Willis had refused to have anything to do with Swain, he expected that he might get the same treatment, even though his sister has a legal right to her own daughter. He decided to kidnap Lily, expecting that they'd be far away by the time the hue and cry died down.'

'Rotter!' Maudie commented.

'Yes, well, that's the sort of man he is. Unfortunately he snatched Polly by mistake. He'd never met his niece and as you know, Mrs Willis dresses the girls alike and they both have flaxen hair. Swain came on the scene in the nick of time, recognized Polly, and intervened.'

'And signed his own death warrant because Smith was afraid he'd talk,' Maudie said sadly. 'But why try to strangle Emma Plummer?'

'By his own admission, Smith took to hanging around the school in the hope of taking Lily. On one occasion he saw the child chatting to the teacher and pointing in his direction. Again, he acted in self-defence. He was afraid that poor Emma would report him to the police, and, since he'd already killed once he had nothing to lose by silencing her.'

'But I still don't understand why Polly didn't run straight home after Smith tried to nab her.'

'She's not saying, but I suspect it was because her parents seemed to be angry with Swain and had forbidden him to see Polly. I expect she thought she'd be blamed for what happened and so decided to lie low for a while.'

'And then there was me, Dick.'

'Ah, yes, Miss Marple! Then there was

you. I think he tried to throw you off the scent by vandalizing your office, as a warning, if you like. When that didn't work he followed you into the churchyard, although now he swears blind that he only meant to frighten you off, not to actually choke the life out of you.'

'Cheek!'

'Well, he did catch you going through his belongings, you know.'

'Trying to find dry clothes for the wretched man!'

'So you say!'

'The worst of it is, it was all so unnecessary,' Maudie said. 'If only he'd gone through the proper channels Ruth could have got her daughter back in the end by legal means, and poor old Swain wouldn't have died. What possesses a man to kill, Dick?'

Bryant shook his head. 'That's a question that the police have been asking since the beginning of time,' he said. 'Are some people born evil, Nurse, predestined to kill? My theory is that we'll see a lot more of this sort of thing in the years to come. In wartime we teach men to kill, even give them medals for doing it, and then we expect them to come back and behave like solid citizens. It doesn't seem natural to me.'

'I'm afraid you may be right. And what happens to Lily now, I wonder?'

'That will be for the courts to decide. A judge may rule in favour of her natural mother, I suppose.'

'Poor little mite. Imagine going thousands of miles away to live with a woman she probably doesn't even remember.'

They were silent for a while, their thoughts sober. 'So that's it, then,' Bryant said at last.

Maudie nodded. 'Yes, I suppose it is.'

He stood in front of her awkwardly, twisting his helmet in his hands. 'I was — er — wondering . . . '

'Yes?'

'I was hoping you might want to go out with me sometime.'

'Really?' This was so unexpected that Maudie didn't know how to respond at first. Instead she smiled at him uncertainly, and waited.

'I thought we might go to the pictures

if anything good comes to Midvale.'

'That would be nice.'

'Actually I fancy one that's been on all this week,' Bryant said. '*Two Years Before the Mast*. It's an adventure story, with Alan Ladd.'

'Oh, is it? I'm not sure if I fancy that.'

'Then what about *My Darling Clementine*, coming next week? It's got Henry Fonda and Victor Mature.'

'That sounds as if it has something to do with Winston Churchill's wife. You know, Clementine, or Clemmie, as I'm told he calls her.'

'No, I believe it's a Western,' he said.

'All cowboys and shoot-outs, then?'

Bryant shuffled his feet. 'Perhaps you'd rather see something romantic, Nurse.'

'For goodness' sake call me Maudie!' she cried. 'And don't assume I only go for romance, just because I'm a woman. I don't like Westerns much, but I don't mind sitting through a ripping adventure yarn, so if you happen to be free this evening I'll be delighted to accept.'

'Really? Shall I come here to collect you?'

'No need for that, since I'll be travelling by bus. I know you don't have a car of your own, and I hardly want to roll up in the Black Maria. What time does the first showing start? I'll meet you outside the Odeon if you'll save me a place in the queue.'

For a long moment they stood beaming at each other, each wrapped in a rosy dream of delights to come. Then the door was flung open, revealing a distraught man.

'Nurse! Nurse! It's started! Can you come? The wife says to tell you the pains are coming every five minutes. Is this bad, or what?'

'I'll be right there, Mr Harkness,' Maudie said, turning to Bryant with a rueful expression on her homely face. 'No rest for the wicked! We'll make it another time, shall we, Dick?'

'I suppose we'll have to,' was his glum reply.

We do hope that you have enjoyed reading this large print book.

Did you know that all of our titles are available for purchase?

We publish a wide range of high quality large print books including:
Romances, Mysteries, Classics
General Fiction
Non Fiction and Westerns

Special interest titles available in large print are:
The Little Oxford Dictionary
Music Book, Song Book
Hymn Book, Service Book

Also available from us courtesy of Oxford University Press:
Young Readers' Dictionary
(large print edition)
Young Readers' Thesaurus
(large print edition)

For further information or a free brochure, please contact us at:

Ulverscroft Large Print Books Ltd.,
The Green, Bradgate Road, Anstey,
Leicester, LE7 7FU, England.
Tel: (00 44) **0116 236 4325**
Fax: (00 44) **0116 234 0205**

Other titles in the
Linford Mystery Library:

THE SUBSTANCE OF A SHADE

John Glasby

Soon after moving into Mexton Grange, an old Georgian country house in the Cotswolds, Alice hears disquieting stories and rumours about her new abode: the previous owners had been driven out by a strange, oppressive atmosphere in the house. It was not as if the house was *actually* haunted — rather, it was as if the house was *waiting to be haunted . . . These five stories of terror and the macabre by John Glasby will tingle the spine on any dark and stormy night.*

THE GLASS HOUSE

V. J. Banis

When Antoinette swindled Margaree out of the old estate on Cape Breton Island, Margaree swore on her mother's grave that she'd win it back. But blocking her ambition are three deadly obstacles: the formidable Antoinette; her treacherous son; and Jean, whom she loves deeply but who hates the old house with all his heart. To win Jean, Margaree would have to give up the estate. The key to it all lies somewhere within the mysterious reaches of the Glass House . . . if Margaree remains alive long enough to find it!